BREAKING ORBIT

SULAYMAN QAZI

Breaking Orbit

Summary: In the midst of a deteriorating world nation, Storm
Raleston is caught in the crossroads of choosing the lesser of two
evils in a conflict that threatens the survival of the human race.

ISBN-13: 978-1535126755
ISBN-10: 1535126752

Text: Garamond; Adventure Subtitles by Pixel Sagas
Cover Illustration by Sulayman Qazi

CreateSpace, Charleston SC

First Printing, 2016

To my mother and father,
Thank you for giving me the pen and paper

CHAPTER ONE

"Questions?" The professor asked. His silver hair stuck up like weeds on a spring morning. I didn't know that he was gazing in my direction. It was as if he was aiming a gun at the class. The clicking of laptop keyboards and flipping notebooks reminded me of home. A student with short, black hair brought herself into the topic of discussion.

"I am confused," she groaned. "So, did The Final Battle begin in the twenty-second or twenty-third century?" I sighed. I thought my gust of wind was quiet, but she flinched. She moved quickly to face me. "What, Storm?"

The professor clucked as if he sampled the brewing conflict, stepping forward.

"It began in the twenty-second century, Jessica," he said.

She slumped back into her seat; I kept my mouth sealed. A cynical response came to mind, but it was too late to express it.

"For those of you who are still confused, it ended in the twenty-third century, which we all know

4

marks the birth of Pangaea. Remember, midnight marks a century of worldwide peace and progress."

"Let's hope that it will also mark its long-awaited death," added a student from the corner of the room. Every man and woman in the class gave him their attention. It was not possible that he could have said such a thing. I came from New York City, and speaking in that way was more than treasonous. I knew that Chicago was a rebellious city, but breaking the law is breaking the law. I bit my lip; the room would have surely not let him survive. Little did I know, the class of young, rebellious students broke into laughter.

"Good one!" shouted one student.

"Preach it!" added another.

Grinning, he was patted on the back by those behind him. I was only here for four days, but this was the first time that I witnessed it. A ringing voice unveiled memories that I previously attempted to bury.

"Chicago is a dangerous city, Storm."

"Neo-Revolutionists brainwash the youth on campus."

"They are recruited to fight for them through the colleges."

"Stop!" the professor struck hand against the silver desk beside him. Some students rolled their eyes while others groaned louder than before.

Why was I here? I never chose to move. I never chose to attend a university of students I didn't understand. They held no care for the history, the effort, the millions of lives that were lost for Pangaea. It should have brought red to their cheeks, but it didn't. Students continued to bicker amongst themselves. After all, they weren't paying for their education. The aging professor arched his back and sighed. This was not the first time that he had to quell a rowdy history class.

If this occurred in New York, the professor would have called in the police. Students would have been strapped in cuffs to pay the consequence. They would then be sent to government centers, rewiring their rebellious heads. It wasn't worth the consequence. Besides, who on Earth yearned for it to be divided? I seemed to have been the only student that respected his frustration.

My heart thumped empathetically, and my fists clenched. I rose from my seat, gritting my teeth. The students glanced at me for a split second and then continued to bicker.

"Shut up!" I barked. Students watched my fury, perhaps getting a fix from it. "What is wrong with you guys, huh?" My legs began to tremble, and I felt my breaths shorten.

"Ask yourself that question. You're the guy with a girl's name!" Jessica said.

The class burst into another round of malignant giggles. I slumped into my seat, blushed. Caught at the crossroads of replying and storming outside the university, I started for the door, utensils, and folders in the cradle of my arm. My legs shook with every step. As I passed the professor, I felt the warmth of his grin. I slammed the door behind me; my stomach fluttered. I leaned on the concrete walls of the building. It hasn't been a week and I wanted to go back.

It was no surprise that the professors greeted me with such compassion since I spoke to them about my transfer from New York. They simply wanted more students to share the same values the older generation represented. Maybe I was wrong for being a conformist, but I stood with what my gut told me. This city was too much to handle. An exit sign hovered above a door on the other end of the hallway, flashing red.

Grandpa's apartment building rested a block away from campus. It was the only place I had, the only home I could plunge my skull in. I wouldn't have dared to breach the boundaries of the university again. My arms pushed open the door, greeting my skin with a warm gust of wind.

"Storm!" shouted a familiar voice. I paused and turned my head. The old professor held out his hand, motioning me to halt. He abandoned his class for me. I thought of a quick response to prevent him from wasting his time.

"I'm just going to go home." I shook my head.

"I know you are, young man," he said, still shaken by what happened. "I'm glad you stepped in."

"You're welcome," I said, glancing at the immunity of the outdoors. A towering Tenbrook Tower stood across the street. It was where I lived. "I should have known more before I moved here." I stepped closer to the vacant street, only to be halted again.

"It's okay if you want to drop the class," he said. "I know you moved here several days ago, but please, do not get comfortable here."

"What do you mean?" I questioned. He stepped even closer to me like he would tell me something I shouldn't repeat.

"Chicago is bound to fall like the other cities. Loyalists like us are fleeing to the capital for a new life. You're the only person I know that had the choice to leave New York."

"My Grandpa wanted cheap rent here," I said. "I could have only objected so much."

"Well, you can always contact me for advice. I wish you the best of luck."

"You too," I replied. He turned back to the class. I knew I wouldn't bother to contact him. He seemed like someone I would sit down and drink coffee with; someone I would ramble my life conflicts to. Fortunately, I wouldn't have to face that situation. I needed to leave this city first.

I walked onto the eerie street, leading me to the parking lot and the entrance to the Tenbrook tower. Each step removed the burden of the university on my shoulders. Grandpa told me that education was key to success, but there would be no success if the student body killed me. As long as I lived with Grandpa, I didn't have to worry about the notion of success.

In a blur, I made my way to the lobby and towards the apartment elevator. Only two people crossed me: two women in suits locking hands. It seemed like the city became emptier with every passing day. Maybe that was why the rent was almost free. Unlike other apartments, the residents of the Tenbrook tower had their own designated elevators. My elevator was conveniently placed by the assistance desk, giving Grandpa and I prioritized access. All elevators had seats with harnesses because elevators only knew to jump up in lightning acceleration or free-fall to ground level.

Bing! The doors pulled up, revealing the signature rust stains on the once reflective walls. I stepped into the elevator, sat on its snug seat, and locked in the harness from above. Maybe elevators contributed to the death of amusement parks. Our elevator needed repairs because it rattled anyone inside. But then, I couldn't have expected much from a cheap apartment.

In a jolt, the door closed and sprang up. My back arched from the pressure. It didn't seem to get better every time I rode it. After several seconds, I filled my lungs with air. The harness unlocked prematurely and sprang up to the opening door. While the elevator door drew up, the smell of red roses and dark chocolate filled the air. It brought the sense of home amid a chaotic life. My sensitive ears detected the candid laughs from a satire show on the hologram display.

"Grandpa, I've had enough!" I said.

"What?" he questioned, standing beside the seat facing the holographic display. His wrinkles under his eyes intensified. His thin patch of gray hair was grasping for dear life. The red, striped shirt he wore represented a style of another era.

"I can't stand it. These students are driving me into insanity." I walked up to the holographic display, watching the characters dance in front of me. "We need to get back to New York. I'm sick of this place."

"Your education is important."

"Education?" I slouched on the seat, pretending to observe the broadcasted show. "The best university here is filled with students who don't even know their history. I can get a degree from these universities based on what I learned from high school."

"You're going to drop out of an easy course?" he asked. I suddenly had the urgency to thump my head on a blunt object.

"Yes," I said, finishing my answer with the hiss of a rattlesnake. "I want to get out of this place while I'm at it."

Grandpa slouched with a smile plastered on his face. He knew how to turn the tables of every situation towards his favor.

"Okay, goodbye," he giggled. The laughs he discarded were like the forced squeals of a dying, rabid animal. In a heartbeat, I knew I had to surrender to his upper hand of the argument.

"This is so annoying!" I cried, dropping myself hands into the soft embrace of the sofa's cushions. The tension between Grandpa and I was never invisible. It was a game of who held more authority: a game I didn't sign up for. I only wished he took my pleas seriously.

"You're going to university whether you like it or not," he said without flinching. He patronized me like a child that relied on his guidance. The thought of a twenty-two-year-old relying on a ninety-three-year-old man for financial support was embarrassing, to say the least. I gazed at the holographic screen, but I remained stuck in the antagonizing train of thought. I needed to prove to Grandpa that I was no longer a child that needed his dependence. I needed to stand for myself and make myself heard.

Grandpa gradually lowered himself to the seat beside me and switched channels to news updates. As an old man, he was one of a small group of people that cared to keep up with the fast-paced world. The broadcaster was a new and inexperienced woman. She stuttered on several words, and her forehead was glimmering with anxiety.

"The five-hundred-pound man was able to climb Mount Everest with little effort. This has surprised many nutritionists, most whom warned the overweight individual prior to making the audacious climb."

I examined the live news clip attentively. The man stood on a pedestal, delivering a speech to several hundred doctors. He gained respect for taking the initiative, the initiative of an audacious risk. If the overweight man took a risk to prove his pride to nutritionists, I had to do something that mirrored it. Mind games were my forte.

The news broadcaster diverted the news to a victorious win by Pangaean forces, a rare update. I continued to ponder the thought of the five-hundred-pound man and his journey. Suddenly, a clever plan came to mind.

CHAPTER TWO

"**G**randpa, I have a question," I said, resting on the sofa

"What do you want?" he asked.

"For once in my life, I want to see the International Celebration. It's a historic day! It marks the one hundred yea-"

"One hundred years of tyranny, and failure." His unruly eyebrows came together, making way to his already wrinkled forehead. "Call me a treasonous man, but I will never let you adhere to a government of supercomputer tyrants."

I groaned as I looked away. "Grandpa, that is exactly what begun the Final Battle. How will a human represent everyone in the world? Only a supercomputer can speak a thousand languages, connect cultures, and spot corruption wherever it is. Humans do just the opposite." I felt proud for rehearsing yesterday's history lesson.

Grandpa shook his head, lifted the hot bowl of ginger tea. He slurped the scorching drink's synthetic flavor.

"You do not know anything. The failed nation of Pangaea is already in the midst collapsing, and everybody knows it," he sneered. The words pierced my honor, slapping me crosswise. Kindness failed, which only meant I had to move to a more drastic measure.

"I am going to the International Celebration in Niamey, and there is nothing you can do to stop me!" I barked. Grandpa beamed his eyes at me. I stood from the dented seat and escorted myself into my bedroom.

"You are making a big mistake, Storm! Niamey is dangerous right now!"

"I am twenty-two. You don't need to baby me anymore!"

I stood up and made way to my bedroom. The hinged compressors shut the door behind. A smell of burnt wood resonated from the walls. I used to pinch my nose, but it hardly bothers me now. I stood head-on towards my mirror. I had natural tiresome eyes with dark circles moving lower with every passing day. My brown eyes were dilated, and the loose, black clothes latching onto me only complimented the void in them. I wore brown hair, but depending on the lighting, it could be confused with black.

"Mirror, I am going to a celebration. What should I wear?" I asked, still trembling from the defiant act against Grandpa. After several seconds of silence, I sighed and peeked behind the mirror. The mirror's power cord sat a foot away from the unplugged socket. I halfheartedly picked up the wire and plugged it into the socket. "Mirror, what should I wear for a celebration?"

"What kind of celebration do you speak of?" the mirror said. It had a tone too soft, too elegant. It made me shiver. Despite its creepiness, the mirror was a helpful tool for shopping, browsing the web, and making video calls.

I am going to a colossal celebration, celebrating the birth of Pangaea."

"Please wait for a connection," the mirror insisted. I was aware the international net was lagging as twenty billion Pangaean citizens attempted to connect on the historic anniversary. Besides, cyber-attacks have swelled the past several months by ruthless Neo-Revolutionaries. *"I found a handsome outfit for you!"*

The mirror's multipurpose display unveiled magenta tights with a blonde, synthetic cotton shirt. The articles of clothing looked like a superheroes outfit, but that was the current trend anyway. Synthetic leather boots had a sharp outline. Whenever I looked at any leather material, I couldn't seem to shake off the fact that it used to be genuine. Hundreds of years ago, people used to purchase leather from some animal's crust. I wonder how they must have worn it without feeling sick.

"I love it! How much does it cost?" I said.

"*Thirty-five credits,*" the mirror replied. I gasped and followed with biting my tongue. "*Storm, would you like me to set the order?*"

"Y-y-yes."

"*I will not submit the order if you are not certain, Storm.*"

"Please, just submit the order before I change my mind."

"*Do not worry, Storm. The transaction is complete, and your order will arrive in approximately two minutes.*"

I moved over to the balcony door of the heated bedroom and planted my hand on the silky, blue window curtain. I pulled the thick curtain aside to survey the skyline of Chicago. The sun was beginning to set as the grey clouds glided towards it. Smog brushed against the window, veiling the tainted, brown Lake Michigan. Grandpa and I were still unpacking in the budgeted apartment on floor one hundred and thirty-two. We were satisfied that we were able to choose the lower levels. Pangaean government policy required all windows above floor two hundred to be sealed and pressured. We could stroll outside the balcony whenever we wished. Unfortunately, this was where most of the toxic smog in the city collected. A breach in the balcony door could have been a life sentence. It was impossible to make my escape from this level. If I had a parachute, I probably would have jumped. The only way to the hovermobile was through the living room.

I filled my lungs and blew out a gust of wind before stepping into the living room. The door opened to the enraged face of Grandpa, waiting outside my door. His hunched back and brown walking stick supplemented the aggressive look. He must have thought it terrified me, but I have seen the same expression since as young as I could remember. Of course, he still thought I was one. He was talking to himself, but the moment we met eyes, he was done rehearsing the lines.

"I am not letting you risk your life for a stupid cause," he snarled.

"Don't get in my way," I said, making way around him. I never spoke to him that way, but the words came out without the filter of thought. I frantically strode into the living room, towards the elevator door. The elevator immediately opened its doors, and I moved into the frosty elevator seat. Grandpa paced across the living room behind me. His walking stick thumped on the floor with every step.

"Stop now, Storm!" he shouted.

I wordlessly hitched on the safety harness over my head. Grandpa was three feet away from the elevator, and he stuck out his shaking, frail hand to prevent the doors from closing.

"Ground level," I demanded as I glanced at his eyes before the doors closed. The look of sorrow and worry lent over to me. I realized this act of defiance had crossed the line, but pride held a higher weight.

Swoosh! The elevator doors shut, and I became weightless. Tranquil two seconds were followed by the sharp slowdown. My pride was left in the apartment above, but I couldn't have stopped what I started. As much as I wanted to turn back, the addicting flow of adrenalin was already rushing. Since I was a child, risks brought life to me. But I never thought these risks could have hurt the most important person in my life, Grandpa.

"You are on the ground level," informed the elevator.

"No way," I murmured. The harness automatically lifted itself over my head. The door lifted, letting commotion and clatter pervade my ears. Hundreds of residents made their way to elevators in the lobby. The sunset rush brought in many into their homes from whatever work they attended. I darted outside the elevator and made way towards the congested crowds. The information desk held most drone delivered packages. Anything light and confidential was sent directly to the apartment's balcony.

I let out a gust of air, realizing an agile character bumped into me from the side. I began to lose my balance, almost tripping on the marble floor.

"Excuse me," I said, turning my head towards the mysterious figure with a wide sombrero covering its face. The magenta tights, blonde long sleeve shirt, and obsidian shoes were oddly familiar.

"Theo?" I kept my voice muffled. The character placed his fingers on the sombrero and pinched it off. His pink, cheeky smile resonated with chutzpah. Tangerine hair hung below his elegant navy blue eyebrows; it was him.

"How do I look, Storm?" Theo asked. I rushed over to him with a grin on my face and put him in a chokehold. I rubbed his hair until strands of orange hair dwindled on the marble floor. "Ouch, Ow, Storm! Stop it!"

"I'm not stopping until you apologize!" I continued.

"I'm sorry for not replying to your calls!" he whimpered. I lifted my hand over his head and my eyes met his grey, sorrowful eyes.

"Where have you been these past two weeks?"

"I was in Mexico for vacation." He threw on the sombrero back onto his head. "Security is getting so bad with travel, the border people asked for proof of…um… what do you call it?"

"Citizenship. By the way, when did you get those clothes, aside from the sombrero?" I questioned, ignoring his routine complaints.

"Today," he said. I grabbed him by his new shirt, against his will, hauling him towards the information desk. The cyborg that sat behind the wooden desks gave an uneasy smile.

"How may I help you today, Storm Raleston?" It asked with curiosity. It was a poor type of curiosity as if it was exaggerating its programmed emotions.

"I would like to know if the delivery drone dropped off my package," I rushed. The cyborg paused momentarily and reached for what was under the desk. While the robot burned daylight, I sighed. The indistinguishable customer service operating system had been used for two hundred years, and its retro appeal was buried with lackluster service.

"Ah, yes! Your package arrived a minute ago, Storm." The cyborg pulled out the lightweight cardboard box.

"Thanks!" I blurted as I swiftly snatched the box from the cyborg's plastic hands.

"What is that?" Theo asked.

'You'll see! It's a surprise!" I smiled. "Sit outside the washroom."

"Okay," he said. I dashed in front the unisex bathroom and pushed open the door to be greeted with the stench of excrement. I held my nose and shut the door behind me. Curiosity ripped opened the box to glance the garments. The attractively packed outfit was waiting for me to use, removing my regret of the steep expenditure. Undressing piece after piece, I felt free. My ears tuned in for any visitors, but the only sound came from the holographic television in the corner of the bathroom.

"In the wake of the one hundredth anniversary of the United Republics of Pangaea, the city centers of Tokyo, Mexico City, and Sao Paulo fell to the ruthless, Neo-Revolutionary terrorists." The holographic news reporter conveyed concern as she delivered the chilling development. *"The Cyber Parliament of Pangaea has declared the provinces of Mexico, Japan, and Brazil as areas to avoid visiting. The suspension of internet and electricity in the provinces will go into effect on the anniversary of Pangaea's formation."*

I stood in front of the bathroom mirror and adjusted the magenta tights onto my waist. I shrugged off the concerning development to observe the beauty of my clothing. A thud on the bathroom door jolted me awake.

"Storm, please hurry!" Theo shouted.

"Okay, okay," I replied. My ears remained attentive towards the hologram display, but my eyes kept gazing at the well-fit outfit.

"The suburbs of Niamey remain in dreadlock, and Neo-Revolutionists push forward to advance into the African province's capital. Despite this, loyal residents of Niamey remain

resilient in continuing the scheduled midnight celebration," the hologram continued. I threw on my skin tight long sleeved shirt and stepped into the snug leather shoes.

"Check it out," I cheered. Theo threw open the door.

"We're wearing the same clothes!" he said. "Of course, we are! Now, let's head out to the International Celebration."

"Which one?"

"The celebration in Niamey," I suggested. He made a silly giggle, but he was quick to notice that I wasn't joining the banter.

"Are you serious?"

"Yeah, let's go." I kept my face stern.

"You're crazy, Storm! Why would you do that?" Pride replaced any rational bone in my body.

"Let's show everyone we know that we have the guts to travel to any corner of the world," I declared. "Especially Grandpa. He thinks I'm some no-good-for-nothing, dependent child."

"Well, you don't have a job, and you would be homeless without him," he said. Although Theo was a friend, he was too stupid to filter out whatever unnerved me.

"I'd rather not be reminded," I said.

"Look, I would just go somewhere safer," he reverted subjects. I watched the way he looked at me as if nothing really seemed to faze him. I was always a prime source of influence on Theo's life, but the influence didn't reach his intelligence. No matter what I did, I knew he would follow suit to the capabilities of his mental capacity.

"Then you're going to miss out on the celebration. Have fun being hurdled up in your apartment." I pushed him aside and opened the door of the restroom. My nose was finally relieved of the stench. I casually strolled towards the exit of the building with my exercise clothing thrown over my shoulder. I heard a familiar clatter from the distance, seeing Grandpa chasing me behind. His walking stick was hovering above the ground.

"Come back here, young man!" he squawked. I darted towards glass exit doors, throwing my hands on them, greeted by a frigid breeze. The sky was dark. Hovermobiles in the distance broke the sound barriers, like an endless stream of fireworks.

I scanned the parking lot for my pink hovermobile, but I was unable to detect it. I didn't quite remember using it for weeks, so I let it collect the dry wind. I didn't let my fault-riddled memory stop me from sprinting into the parking lot. I threw my wrist in the air, triple tapping my wristband, hearing a faint hovermobile honk. I turned my head to the sound to spot the old hovermobile several feet away, hidden from plain sight. The clunker was bought by my grandfather when I was a child, but it was eventually passed onto me because Grandpa walked to 'keep his youth' as he walked back and forth to work. Its green headlights were a retro style. The artificial intelligence was a technological feat for its time. I darted towards the clunker and tapped my wrist twice. The scissor door opened. I threw myself into the snug seating and double tapped my wristband to choke the doors to a close. I was not sure if the goose bumps on my arms were from the rush of flight or the cool Chicago breeze.

"Hello, Storm. Where shall I take you today?" the artificial intelligence said, retaining an almost identical tone as the mirror.

"Ta-take me to Cyborg Square, Niamey, of the African Provence" I rushed, finishing my sentence from numbed lips. While I waited for the artificial Intelligence to recognize my collage of words, I was interrupted by thuds against the window. My heart skipped a beat, and my breath suspended. A still figure stood outside the hovermobile. I glanced to my left, only to observe a black silhouette lean on the vehicle. He was hunching, thumping the window beside me. My leg began to bounce on the toe, and I cursed under my breath. This was it; I was caught. My plan to prove Grandpa of my independence was a failure. The thumps became more frantic and assertive by the second.

"What do you want?" I shook. Silence briefly fell between the windows that separated me from the mysterious figure.

"It's Theo!" he replied. I let out an anxious breath and slid down the window. The light that beamed from instrument panel reflected on Theo's sharp cheekbones. "Let me in the car!" he requested, "Your grandpa is running like a crazy person!"

"Hop in, then!" I replied. I double tapped my wrist, and scissor doors elevated themselves for him. Theo darted for the passenger seating and hurdled into the passenger seat.

"Your grandpa looked like he wanted to kill you," he giggled.

"Shut up, Theo." I punched the launch button. "I thought you were Grandpa."

The clunker chugged and hoisted itself off the ground. I assumed the half empty battery would take us there, yet it struggled to rush off the ground.

My eyes scanned the parking lot for the frail man. I saw him at the entrance of the towering apartments. After several tense seconds, he spun around back into the doors of the building with his head hung low. We darted onto the virtual path, an imaginary road in the sky made only for hovermobiles. While I fastened my safety harness, Theo watched me.

"I just wish my parents were here to see this," I blurted, continuing my gaze forward. Silence broke in the cabin as the hovermobile drifted towards the International Bullet Express Highway.

"You have me, Storm." Theo placed his hospitable hand on my shoulder. I turned my head towards his solemn expression and cracked a grin.

"Fasten your harness, Theo," I replied. Merging onto the express in the speed of a bullet, we soared to Africa to witness the celebration of a century. I would be the man that dared to climb the mountain, despite opposition. However, this was no mountain; this was a warzone.

CHAPTER
THREE

"I recommend that you do not take the exit to Niamey," the artificial intelligence said.

I punched the override button. It became a broken record player, aware of the pending danger since we recharged the hovermobile's battery in Bermuda.

"Will it ever shut up?" Theo asked.

"Be patient. We're almost there," I replied. I glimpsed over my shoulder and observed another vehicle with bumper stickers in a foreign language.

In the two hours of flight, thousands of hovermobiles with differing origins and destination came into our perception. The obsidian ocean swayed fifty feet below the virtual track, darkened in the moonlight. I cracked a grin with the emergence of a treasured memory.

"What's so funny?" Theo observed.

"Well," I said, "I don't know if I should tell you."

"Tell me," he insisted, poking my shoulder with his elbow. Theo always got what he wanted, especially when I placed the unspoken on the table.

"This might sound really stupid, but when I was thirteen, I thought I was going to crack the code of the virtual path. I would let all the hovermobiles free. People would manually control them, and they would fly away into space." The nervous grin continued to latch onto me past its due point.

"Hey, when I was thirteen, I thought I was going to get a girlfriend," Theo replied. I burst into laughter as Theo glared at me.

"It's very clear that nothing has changed in nine years," I giggled.

"And as for you?" he refuted. I muffled my humor at the truth of the remark. Theo swiped his orange hair with the back of his soft hand and aimed his eyes towards the holographic figure which displayed the route.

"The exit comes in three minutes!" he announced. Theo's rich character and animated expressions had always electrified the environment around him. This time, however, the hair that sat on the back of my head stood up from what I was seeing. Before I could express my concern, a squeal from the artificial intelligence issued its final warning. *"Mr. Raleston, you are entering a stage three militarized zone. In the case of a mandatory evacuation from the following province, you must enter a security code so I may be able to send you to a safe location,"* it said. I hesitated, hardly moving a muscle. I had the decision to continue my navigation forward and ground in Europe, like most foreigners. I also held the decision to remain committed to the plan that I sketched. My hands were frozen. From the looks of it, it was a decision between cowardice and courage.

"Storm, you're taking forever, put in the code!" Theo groaned. I was glad Theo took partial responsibility for it. I raised my left hand and drew it to the surface of the keypad.

Beep, beep, beep, beep. The holographic keyboard disintegrated from sight. A final word came from the speakers.

"Stay safe, Mr. Raleston." My back was not lying on the plush seating; I didn't want to. The virtual path that led to the African continent held lifeless lights. There was no moon, no stars to guide us. Instead, I crossed my fingers.

"Really, Storm? One-one-one-one?" Theo questioned.

"I had to make it easy to remember!" I said. "Who remembers passwords anymore?"

Inertia from the exit's turn pushed me to the wall of the cabin. The Bullet Express's path was no longer powered here. Habit always brought the Pangaean government to sanction electricity to fallen provinces. Halting power to a province that had not fallen yet was premature, almost questionable. Silence pierced the air, with the hum of the hovermobile pushing us to a destination that held uncertainty in its palm. A dark ocean was replaced with the lifeless African desert. Dead trees and skeletal remains of animals littered the dark sand.

"Theo, are you sure this is a good idea?" I asked.

"I thought you were the one that wanted to do this," he replied.

"I know, but I've been thinking it over, and I'm worried about you. I don't want you to feel unsafe."

I was petrified, but blanketing the fear seemed like the most rational decision. Theo and I were adrenaline junkies, looking for the next opportunity to keep our blood flowing. I was not going to let that identity be questioned. Unfortunately, the goose bumps on my arms did not come from the cool, night desert.

"I thought it over too, and I actually want to do this now." Theo smiled. He touched his eye several times like something was lodged in the corner of it. After he glanced at his reflection in the mirror, I was led to undoubted suspicion.

"Theo, are you recording this?" I raised my voice, observing the thin, red outline on his eye. "I'm not okay with this!"

The contact that Theo wore was another piece of tech savvy equipment that he obsessed over. It could upload a live stream of video from the cornea of an eye. His social media accounts were tied to the eyepiece.

"Come on, don't be a buzz-kill!" Theo said. He looked directly at me, recording me. I didn't want to be seen by others, especially those who questioned my choices. The live feed from Theo's contacts could have been seen by all his friends, or anyone, including Grandpa.

"Just don't look at me!" I barked. The clunker begun to halt its breaking of the sound barrier as the horizon of Niamey glimmered in the darkness. The joy of celebration swept over me with variations of colors surrounding the horizon. A smile cracked on my face and ricocheted onto Theo.

"Look at how beautiful it looks," I said, pointing forward. We were gliding closer to the outskirts of the city. The lightings display made unprecedented dances. Red and orange spectacles illuminated from the city center. This celebration must have spanned across the city and into its outskirts. I observed and observed until my gut began to twist. Before I could vomit the panic, Theo choked out the visuals.

"Those are fires!" he cried with a cracking voice. The series of blazes were symbolic of liberty and freedom by the Neo-Revolutionist forces. We zipped over the damaged infrastructure that the insurgency caused. A droplet of anxious sweat slid across my cheekbone and dug itself under my chin. Pangaean flags marked the tall structures that surveyed the historic city. Vertically striped, the three colors of the flag were engrained in my robust pride. The left, pink stripe stood for world love and universal respect. The yellow stripe in the middle of the flag stood for global prosperity and wealth. Finally, the last installment of the flag was the black strip. Black stood for strong universal unity, law, and order. The city center seemed to be the stronghold for Pangaean forces. It was under siege.

"I'm sure it's safe here," I said. Theo's paralyzed hand gripped onto the hugging harness.

"Safety is an illusion," he replied, whispering. Parking zones with several hovermobiles lured the autopilot to glide back down.

Signs drafted in the Hausa language projected across the open-air parking zone in the deadlocked city. We descended into the parking zone and hit the ground with a rattle. Another jolt of anticipated adrenaline rushed through my blood. I stretched my arm into the center console for my translation contacts. They could change any words to English, which is an undoubtedly better accessory to bring, besides, the contacts Theo wore were incapable of doing that.

"Ouch!" I cried. A stinging prickle on the metal box which housed my contacts stung my fragile finger. Theo silently chuckled, but he quelled his humor when I darted my eyes to his. I opened the troublesome box to observe the contacts were in full charge. Individually placing each contact onto my dry eyes, the moisture in them hazed my vision. I blinked several times before I glanced at the Hausa sign that faced the parking zone. Words transformed into the English standard.

"Free Parking brought to you by the Pangaean government," I read aloud. "Sweet!"

"Give me a pair," Theo insisted.

"That's disgusting," I said.

He mumbled in objection. I plucked out the small earbud from the container and jabbed it into my eardrum. It would translate every Hausa word spoken. I double tapped my wristband, and the doors of the hovermobile creaked up. I clipped both of my leather shoes onto the parking zone's polished floors.

While I elevated my head above the parked vehicle, blood rushed throughout my soaring legs. I surveyed the sky rise buildings that dominated the landscape of Niamey. Smog blanketed the atmosphere, shielding my view to the tips of the sky rises. The night sky dimmed as the dawn of midnight lurked about. Theo stood in awe of the beauty.

"To think that this was once the capital of poverty and hunger is kind of shocking," Theo pondered out loud. I was surprised he even knew such fact. The remark triggered my last memory in the historic city. I traveled on a field trip with my Hausa Language Class several years ago. The African Museum of History in Niamey dangled a photograph of a boy in the early twenty-first century who suffered the age-old effects of starvation. His bones were frail, and his face, malnourished.

Territorial divisions prevented the world to care for one another. The chilling caption in the eerie museum disclosed the cause of his death. The boy died of disease before he was fifteen. Fortunately, that no longer happens. Now, the leading cause of preventable death is the ruthless insurgency.

I began to stroll towards the central street that led to Cyborg Square. The hovermobile doors clicked shut behind us. With every step, the sounds of cheers of an exuberant congregation polluted the air around us. A gust of heated wind that whisked against my skin had a chilling antecedent. Empty solar paneled streets that we crossed resembled an abandoned gem. Despite the tainted, hideous world we lived in, Niamey was making changes for a greener Earth. Unfortunately, those changes were reverting. Cracks in the ground must have been from the bombings. Theo was walking in silence as he seemed more fascinated than terrified. For the first time, we were not in sync. We turned the last final of the square and small crowd of roughly five thousand stood in Cyborg Square. A hologram of immense size towered over the square, standing defiantly.

"Where are most of the people?" Theo questioned.

"Clearly, they fled," I replied.

"Today is a significant day. One hundred years of peace, and global tranquility," roared the holographic figure from the center of the square. Its blue, spotless suit harmonized the grey, sharp handlebar mustache and slicked back hair. Brown, virtual eyes were plastered with defiance and pride. A grin spelled confidence for the citizens that watched below. The computerized president who addressed the buoyant citizens resembled an African man in his mid-fifties for the Nigerian province. This was a stark difference from the Caucasian form he represented in the province of the Americas. Whatever form he took, he hasn't aged a day in one hundred years. He continued after the pause, *"One hundred years of scientific advancements, prosperity, and development, but the Neo-Revolutionists want to throw us in the dark ages of war, poverty, and corruption!"*

The crowd of loyal citizens roared in agreement. Daredevils, such as Theo and I, represented a quarter of the congregation. Daredevils arrived for social media popularity and respect from their home communities. We were respected as soldiers because human soldiers were a thing of the past. Neo-Revolutionaries, of course, were humans, but very stupid ones. They would risk their lives over an old cause that had no weight in the modern would.

"*We will not bear the brunt of these malignant actions. We will do everything in our power to keep Pangaea from the offensive of Neo-Revolutionists! We will be victorious!*" Theo and I continued to stride towards the clustered square until something in the sky caught my attention. It was the smog, brushing away. Something was chasing it away. Glistening stars watched at the congregation below. The tranquility was almost a message from a divine force. Gazing above without another word spoken, crowds of desperate citizens stood in the apprehension of what was to come. The holographic president that stood taller than the ancient Statue of Liberty looked skywards with the city dwellers. It was silly; why would a hologram care see something that it couldn't?

Suddenly, a rupture pushed me from behind. A deafening blast ushered a tremor, which caused Theo to latch onto me instinctively. Tranquility immediately recaptured the square; I winced.

"What was that?" I attempted to speak, but couldn't hear myself. Solar paneled flooring began to crack. Its thick plastic seemed flimsier than the glass itself. My legs shook with the ground, and before I could take in the magnitude of the situation, I was no longer holding my balance. High-pitched ringing occupied the environment around me. It was rubbing my nerves like drilling a hole in the eardrum. Agony clenched every muscle to the bone. I yanked the earbud out, but the ringing continued to deafen me.

My eyes choked closed, I forced myself to stand. I snapped a glimpse at the towering hologram. It stood still and silenced. The broadcasting signal to Niamey was either fractured, or the president had no more resolutions to offer the desperate people. Whatever it was, my numb feet tried to rush from the scene. Daredevils equipped with patriotic clothing pushed against me, fleeing the city's square. Their faces were plastered with chaos and terror.

Desperate city dwellers remained cemented onto the floors of the city; their pride remained with them. They must have been used to this sound, but it was beyond what I expected from a conflict. I felt a distinct tug on my shoulder as Theo magnetized himself to the clunker resting several hundred feet away.

"Storm, we need to leave now!" he shook. His grey, dilated eyes were more than glossy. His hands clenched firmly onto my arm while he struggled to haul my numbed body towards the road.

I was thirsty to witness what atrocity occurred in the vast distance. The ringing was replaced by the sounds of Pangaea military hovercrafts, gliding gracefully onto the outskirts of the square. Cyborg military personnel darted out of the jets and rounded up defiant Pangaeans for evacuation. It was so fast, too fast for me to comprehend.

Before I turned my head towards the resting hovermobile, I saw a desperate mother who was dragged into the military jet; her weeping child was latched to her grasp. My earbud lied lost in the crowds, but after several months of learning the Hausa language, I was able to understand the mother's pleas.

"Take my child! I want to die here! I want to die here!" she cried.

CHAPTER
FOUR

"*M*r. *Raleston, you will arrive at the Lagos Military Base of Pangaea, briefly.*" The security code activated, and we lifted from the parking zone.

I looked over to Theo who latched onto the flimsy handle as we lifted from the parking lot. The hovermobile's rockets roared, preparing for acceleration. We were an open target in a shifted warzone.

Suddenly, a luminescence ricocheted from the dashboard, hypnotizing me from buckling my harness. I turned to Theo, who was lifelessly situated in the presence of the radiating light. He shaded the shimmering light from my view. The light grew exponentially, and then it disappeared. Something about the visual display reminded me of a video clip I saw in my history class. It reflected the effects of warfare in the twenty-second century. The clip displayed a radiation bomb capable of dosing anyone in its sight with malignant waves, without damaging the infrastructure. As always, assets were valued with more weight than human lives. It was a gentle killer, killing thousands before the establishment of the nation. It was a weapon so deadly, I never had the gut to name it.

"Theo, what was that?" I placed my hand on his arm. My other hand was latched onto the harness, but those fingers were crossed. The curiosity seemed to slow time down. We were in mid-air, and I was waiting for the vehicle to move.

"It-it-it," Theo stuttered. The hovermobile pushed forward and shot us into the brace of the cushioned seating. I forced out a breath. An overwhelming pressure from the artificial intelligence prompted a cruel outcry in the engine.

"It..." I choked for air, "...what?"

"It looked like a radiation bomb," Theo said. He looked at me, and a single tear rolled down the right side of his cheek. His right eye was bloodshot, and his left hand remained clenched onto the handle. The pink glow on his pale skin illuminated.

"Shit," I said, my heart thumping. A throbbing ache struck the core of my head. I had to do something; I had to find safety. I placed both fingers on my temples and pressed gently.

An atomic bomb's mushroom cloud rested in the distance, obliterating what was left in the suburbs. The radiation was in the city center, slowly killing away whoever remained. Illustrated crevices in the sandy hills captivated my attention. I continued to focus on the ground fifty feet below and pondered the outcome of the situation. I couldn't find myself to believe I witnessed. The replayed episode of the woman who wanted to sacrifice herself in the city distracted my view until a series of virtual lights in the distance captivated my attention.

"Look at the path. We're getting there," I said, trying to sound comforting. I didn't want him to know that he had little time before the radiation killed him.

"Storm, I just want to go home," Theo insisted. He covered his right eye with his quivering hand. Witnessing him suffer like that made me feel like I had a hole in my chest.

"I can't do that even if I wanted to," I said. "The computer is in full control now, and you need to be treated for radiation exposure." I kept watching him carefully. Theo sighed and turned his head back to the side window.

"Does it hurt?" I asked.

"No, it's just sensitive right now," he replied. I scanned the virtual path for hovermobiles, failing to find the faintest sign of life. We merged onto the single lit virtual path to the neighboring Pangaea military base. The silence remained. I assumed it was because I was temporarily impaired to hear.

"No, no, no," Theo said. He removed the contact from his left eye and stored it inside the contact storage box. "It's going viral."

"The infection is going viral?"

"No, the video feed... fifty... fifty million," he said. "This was not how I wanted to get viewers."

I lifted my hand and patted his stiff shoulder. "Theo, everyone at home is goi-"

"No, forget about the popularity! The military dropped a nuclear bomb on an entire section of a city! And then, they dropped a radiation bomb on what was left! Think of how many people were still there!" His howling pinched my tender eardrums.

"I'm sorry, you're right," I replied. His hefty breathing from the howling spoke urgency. I visualized the moment of the nuclear explosion and the mandatory evacuation of city dwellers. I caught the correlation between both episodes, but I was not willing to scorn my national pride. Since my birth, I was a patriot of my beloved Earth. I wanted answers, but pinning the great nation was uncalled for. I continued to ponder the magnitude of the situation until Theo leaned forward to the console of the hovermobile.

"Computer, where are we?" he asked.

"You are in the province of Nigeria and on-route to The Military Base of Lagos. You will arrive at your secured destination in approximately seventy seconds," the automated system replied. The bright, cool lighting of the military base was distinguishable on the horizon. Sailing closer to our sanctuary, I let go a sigh of relief.

"We can get checked up here and leave before the sun goes up," I said. Theo failed to respond, gazing out his window regretfully. The sinister silence continued to echo throughout the highway while the clunker slowed towards the exit. Ample in size, the concrete barriers of the base touched the clouds. Several hundred feet from the secure borders of the base, the hovermobile jolted, launching us forward. The jerk derived a whiplash on my fragile neck. A headache was now diverted to a sharp jabbing in my neck.

"Ouch!" I whimpered. I placed my hand on the back of my tender neck. Theo placed his hand on the back of his neck and mocked my injury.

"Owie, I didn't adjust my harness!" His orange hair bounced with fury.

"Shut up, Theo!" I roared. "Computer, what was that?"

The clunker continued to slow down, gliding closer to the sealed entrance of the base. Surveillance bots glided around us and shot a blinding, cold light at the old clunker. Silence fell onto the cabin for several seconds, until a response issued from the base.

"Hello! My name is Jem. I am going to be assisting you while you seek refuge in base premises." The soft transition of words and high-pitched tone that rang in my ear resembled a human. *"The jolt you handled was our takeover of your vehicle's artificial intelli-"*

43

"Are you a human?" Theo interrupted. Several seconds of silence pierced the uneasy atmosphere.

"Please identify yourselves, so we may offer you accommodation." The mysterious, feminine voice failed to respond. Theo glanced at me; I stretched my eyes towards him. My neck was too impaired for drastic twists.

"I'm Storm Raleston, the owner of this vehicle. You injured me, and I need medical attention," I replied.

"Please wait. We have been waiting for you too," the voice responded.

Theo glanced at me with an unfamiliar expression. His well-groomed eyebrows curved up with symmetry. Clinging concrete gates broke the seal to reveal soldiers in black suits and masks. Standing together in an air locked line, their black uniforms reflected the strong national value of unity. They tucked their identity behind the aim of what seemed to be a rifle, barbing it towards us. My breath froze, and I raised both hands in the air; Theo followed suit. In the several seconds the vehicle remained idle, the cool temperate cabin was suddenly sweltering. I continued to hold my breath as Theo's heavy breathing polluted the sound of tense silence. Step by step, the soldiers stepped back and continued to lock on the target. My heart pounded heavily against my chest.

A gentle acceleration glided the vehicle through the entrance, and the gates closed behind. Forcefully, my eyes scanned the amplitude of distance behind the men. Hundreds of black, armored hovercrafts parked in channeled structure. I returned my gaze to the threatening strangers in uniform. I shut my eyes under the concealment of harrowing fear.

"Both of you seem anxious," the tone amplified from the cabin's speakers. *"Don't worry. The soldiers will only hurt you if you try something stupid."*

"That didn't help," I whispered under my breath. The clunker chugged as it lowered to the ground. It made its signature, blatant whine.

"Keep both of your hands up and exit the vehicle."

"Okay, okay," I said, double tapping my wrist above my head; my aching shoulders cramped. The doors launched up in unison with the unlocked safety harness. I was once again greeted by a frigid breeze. The hair on the back of my neck rose. I stepped onto the concrete pavement like it was a minefield. The soldiers continuously aimed in silence, like a hunter in preparation to prey. Every breath I took was short lived.

Boop-Beep! I glanced above at the source of the sound. Scanner bots glided above, giving its melodic gesture of consent. Weapons immediately clattered as they lowered their gaze. I lowered my arms, and the satisfying sensation of blood flow made its way to my numb hands.

I looked at Theo as he stood stiffly behind the vehicle. It would be more than necessary for me to protect him if he was endangered. Theo irritated me more than complied, but I loved him too much to lose him by any means.

The soldiers marched on opposite sides which revealed a woman in a pink uniform. A thick, purple afro complimented her black skin. She smiled with confidence and glided towards my direction. Her purple boots clattered against the concrete floors. She stuck out her right hand and locked eyes with mine. I immediately held out mine as our hands met. Her hand was cold but soft.

"Hello Storm, my name is Jem Hata. I am the commander of this base." She had a firm grasp, enough to strangle someone. The way she looked at me seemed as if she knew me or something about me. Her purple eyeliner represented a position of authority, and the crevices on the side of her eye disclosed her experienced age. She seemed to disguise her mid-forties age. "I was communicating with you just a moment ago," she added. I pursued to break the dry seal between my lips.

"I'm so sorry," I said. "We were automatically brought here because this is the only safe place aside from Niamey." I shook my head, pretending to resent the decision.

"I'm aware. Your friend's video feed went viral, and you were the star of that video." She flashed her eyes at Theo as if he didn't matter. "I know you have many questions, but both of you must follow me."

Jem strode into the depth of the base. We held no other option other than to follow her lead. Theo wrapped his arms around himself, repelling the unusually chilly breeze. Footsteps of cyborg soldiers and their welcome lurked behind.

"We need medical assistance," I pleaded. "Can you help us?"

"Don't worry; we will take care of that," she said.

"Where are we going?" Theo asked with a sliver politeness. He must have feared the woman, but of course, we never shared our weaknesses with each other.

"Headquarters," she replied. Jem slowed her pace as we approached the line of military hovercrafts which spanned for a mile. I couldn't trust her, but meeting the commander of the base was the slightest bit assuring. She motioned to the towering structure that sat two miles into the base's depth. Behind the tower, the borders continued for several miles. From the corner of my eye, a militarized hovermobile gliding a foot from the floor rushed to Jem's disposal. It had darkly armored plating and blinding headlights. A deep humming of the engine disclosed the power of the vehicle. The front door lifted for Jem, and the back doors opened for her honorary guests; the vehicle halted beside her feet.

"There's our ride," Jem said. My neck throbbed as I lowered my head to situate myself into the dark, leather seating.

"Ow!" I reacted, placing my hand on the side of my neck. In a display of agony for Jem, I clenched my eyes. Theo sat right next to me, caressing his shoulder to mine. The doors shut closed, and metal body roared towards the headquarters. Jem twisted her head to observed my exaggerated expression.

"Your neck is in pain?" she asked, tilting her head to the side.

"Yes...it is," I replied. Theo nudged me to speak on his behalf. "Also, my friend was exposed to radiation. His eyes are bloodshot."

"If you want to be treated, your friend needs to identify," Jem said, reaching into the small pockets of her vest.

"That is Theo, Theo Calbrin," I said. She nodded her head as if she already knew our credentials.

"I'm glad you two can comply." Her hand pulled away from the pockets, and she reached out to me. I lifted my hand and opened it for her to drop the mysterious item. Two pills dropped onto my hand. Centimeter thick, the pills weighed on my palm. I have tried all sorts of medicine in my life, but this was something abstract. Theo must have known, and so I trusted his take on it.

"What is in this?" I asked.

"These are extremely expensive pills," she responded. "Nano-bots inside the pills should heal you from any obscurity in several hours. They will stay in your system for several days."

"What are these called?" Theo questioned, taking one from my hand. "I have never heard of these."

"Just take it." Jem pressed her head towards us, condensing the air.

"Okay," Theo replied. As far as we knew, it was wiser to trust the government official. Theo drove the pill into his mouth. I hesitated to take the mysterious medicine but quickly plopped it into my mouth as she locked eyes with mine.

The large, tasteless thing scratched my throat as I consumed it with nothing but spit. Theo struggled to consume the pill and his Adam's apple yo-yoed. I gazed through the window to avoid Jem's uneasy eyes. The hovercrafts that we passed became distorted in the speed of the travel, or that was what my eyes believed. I began to sway back and forth as nausea swept over my body. It could have not possibly been the pill. It was in my system for only several seconds, too fast for any reaction. Deafness ensued, and my heart endeavored to continue pounding. I gasped for air to attempt a cry for help, but I was unable to sound my plea.

Lifelessly slouching beside me, Theo collapsed. His frail body twitched several times and foam poured from his mouth. Before I shut my eyes in surrender, I caught glimpse of Jem's crooked smile.

CHAPTER
FIVE

Pressure on my shoulder blades squeezed against my spine. My eyes pleaded to stay shut, but I wrestled with curiosity. I opened my eyes to a blinding white light. I tried to question what had occurred before I fell unconscious, but the bright environment distracted the thought. I threw my tongue around my mouth and sampled the taste of bitter saliva. I was asleep for several hours from the taste of it. The rugged bedding that pressed against my back stiffened my lying position. Memories were carefully piecing together like the emergence of bloodroots after a winter blizzard. Theo, Jem, the war, the bombs, the medicine; I was beginning to remember it all.

I lifted my hand from the warm blanket and placed it on my stiff neck. I frantically pressed my finger against my neck in search of the sharp throb, but I was unable to find it.

The serene atmosphere persuaded me to continue my rest, but the whereabouts of Theo held me from detachment. I flexed my abdomen, aspiring to lift my chest from the thin bedding. Fatiguing effects from whatever it was remained rooted in my system. I threw my right foot on the cool tiled flooring and pushed my arm against the single bed.

I gave all the push could produce to launch myself on my aching feet. I shivered, feet sensing the intolerable floor. Goose bumps formed on my lanky arms. My yellow, nano-fiber shirt hardly covered me. I clutched the blanket and encased myself as I swayed back and forth. A small table that sat beside me in my slumber held a silver cup and a note. I seized the note and lifted it towards my hazed vision. The white paper featured black, handwritten words; it lost its toneless texture in my grasp.

"Drink up, you must be tired," I read. Stretching for the cumbersome, silver cup, I lobbed the note on the bed. The thick, blue mixture in the cup had a familiar aroma while I lifted it to my frigid nose. "Adrenalin Juice?" I questioned. Analyzing the cup, I rattled the sweet muck. Considering the last episode of lavish medicine, I didn't trust what was in here. The last time I savored this kind of drink was two months ago. Since the province of England was the first to fall, its prominent Adrenalin Factory fell too. Billions around the world were unable to go to the work without the energizing contents it offered.

During the tiresome age, I failed to pay attention in my classes. I had to turn to ancient mixture of coffee for a mild boost in energy. Neo-Revolutionaries sold the muck on the black market for two hundred times the original price, which only landed into the palms of the wealthy class. I analyzed every inch of the blue liquid before I devoured it. Lifting the cool cup to lips, the sharp smell of the Adrenalin Juice moisturized my dry mouth. The lukewarm mixture landed on my tongue, sparking nostalgia. Its synthetic blueberry flavor clung tightly to my taste buds, while the mixture warmed my arid throat. I shut my eyes, relishing the sweet taste I had yearned for. Before the last drop traveled into my system, I was awoken by a sound.

"Wake up soldier!" Jem croaked from the corner of the room, jolting my muscles. Her crooked smile seemed frozen since I fell into unconsciousness. Slanted teeth revealed a cloaked tongue. "You were sleeping for twelve hours." She glanced at her purple watch. I lowered the emptied cup onto the table and clutched the blanket that cocooned me. The spirit of the drink began to resume a part of me that was resting for too long. I was more awake than I had to be.

"What happened? Why am I here? Where is Theo?" I shrieked.

"Take one step back, Storm," Jem said. Her thin eyebrows rose. "The pill set you both asleep to repair your injuries. I believe Theo is awake by now. I'll be discussing with the both of you shortly."

"What?" I said. The thought of Grandpa came to mind, and I shivered under the warmth of the blanket.

"Let's get out of this room so we can discuss everything," she said. "I promise both of you will be home before you know it." My feet remained planted on the frigid floor. She strode to the white door but seemed surprised when she glanced at my stiff resilience. "If you move from that spot, you will see Theo," she added.

I moved to the door. It released a gust of heat into the room. It was like standing next to a fireplace when the sky drizzled snow. A well-decorated room was on the other side of the door. Jem led the way to hospitality.

"This is where I live, on the top floor of headquarters." She gestured to the glass-ceiling dome, which revealed the piercing sun. Red walls held quotes in the several state-sanctioned languages. I leaped into the spacious room; my feet embraced the warm carpeting.

"Where was I sleeping?" I asked. Jem smiled and scratched her nose.

"You were in the emergency room. I would freeze in there for hours when we had air raid warnings because of the Neo-Revolutionists."
She strode past me and turned towards the array of brown sofas. Over one hundred sofas made a circle

around the spacious room. A hefty hologram projector hung from the peak of the dome.

"The walls of that room could stand the most cynical of weapons," she added. I strolled to the nearby seat and collapsed in its warm embrace. The adrenalin rush prevented me from enjoying the relaxation, inducing my leg to bounce on my toe. Jem sat twelve seats away, gazing past the scenic window. With a bright, clear horizon, I would never want to leave a room like this. Suddenly, I snapped back to my consciousness.

"Where is Theo?" I asked. Before Jem could reply, I felt a rough tug on my shoulder. I glanced up as Theo towered me from behind the seat.

"I felt like I was in a sauna," Theo panted. I jumped from my seat and leapt towards Theo. I latched onto him like roots to dirt.

"You're okay!" I sighed, finally able to let go. The thin, soft blanket drifted on the carpeted flooring, alongside worry.

"I am feeling great!" Theo replied. I didn't want to let go of him, but that was before I felt his soaking shirt. Theo continued to hold onto me. He squeezed until I forced the last breath from my lungs.

"You're really sweaty," I patted his back and pulled him towards the pair of seating. His hair drooped, and his pale face shone. I brushed my moist hand on the plush, brown sofas. In the same seat, we sat together. I was never going to let him loose again, even if it meant I had to risk my life.

"He was in the heating room," Jem pointed towards Theo.

"You couldn't have stuffed us in any worse place, could you?" Theo said.

Jem began to laugh, but it sounded forced. Maybe she has not laughed for a long time.

"Maybe," she replied. I watched his dilated black pupils which annexed the remainder of his magnetizing grey eyes. My back leaned back, whispering to him while still facing Jem. She could have thought I was commenting on her, but perceptions could be deceiving.

"Did you drink it too?" I asked.

"Yeah...where did they get it from?" he whispered back.

"I wouldn't ask." I immediately shrugged off the lightheartedness as I turned to Jem for more serious matters. She held a suspicious look, but I didn't know her well enough to sense it.

"Jem, we really want answers about what's going on right now," I cleared my throat. "We really want to know what happened in Niamey." She lowered her wrist and turned to me with her legs crossed.

"I assume you are interested in history?" she asked. I hopped in my seat, interested in the mention of it.

"Of course, in a matter of fact, I am a student of history...or was."

"Okay, that is good enough. Now, let's think of what happened over one hundred years ago. Nations were far beyond divided, giving way to conflicts that led to chaos. These are things you know, right?" Jem turned around and snapped her finger three times in the air.

"Tea is being prepared," an automated voice came from a distance. I leaned in to observe the bar across the room, where a cyborg prepared the drink. It was turned against me, but its human like characteristics demanded maintenance. Black hair dangled from the back of the bot's head, and an apron hung from the tip of the spine.

"Humans became so materialistic, no one wanted to die in battle for a national cause," Jem continued. "Heck, and ninety percent of Pangaean armed forces are cyborgs. Aside from that, an ancient organization, known as The United Nations drafted a resolution that would change the world, forever." She paused to dart her eyes to every corner. "Resolution, Pangaea. A resolution to reconnect the world's continents as the historic supercontinent itself. Half of the world's nations adopted the resolution while the weaker half collapsed in the dust of history. Guess what we did? Annex the other half. While this was occurring, a genius team of computer programmers created the President, Judiciary, and Virtual Council."

I dug my elbow into the snug armrest, captivated by her fluctuating tone. Something about the way she spoke gave me goose bumps. Theo slouched and sighed. "When a computer runs the world, it bears no corruption, no linguistic, racial, or cultural bias. The world remains loyal to the supercomputer government, and the government establishes loyalty to all citizens around the globe." She paused in hesitation but continued in a lowered tone. "I am a military commander, but I am also entitled to my own genuine opinions." She tapped her wristband several times, maybe a code.

Click! The holographic projector pointed down; it was disconnected. Maybe she wanted to save power. Maybe she did not want anyone to hear from the only live connection in the room. She stood from her seat and glided across the obsidian carpeting to sit beside me. She carried an uneasy environment, burdening those around her; including Theo and me. She sat on the plush seating and crossed her legs again, leaning towards me. Theo pressed against my back, leaning from the other side to hear what secret she had to offer.

"The programmers that created this government knew it was bound to collapse," she said. "Before the United Nations dissolved, one of the programmers gave a speech to the world leaders. She spoke of how 'Resolution Pangaea' was only a temporary solution for world peace." Squeaks on the carpet flooring paused her prematurely.

"Your tea is ready, ma'am," the cyborg announced several feet away. Its steps were fluid and natural. Its squinted eyes represented a model of precise designing, while its soft dimples consisted of a contagious smile. Its hand grasped onto blue mug with care.

"Thank you," Jem replied, while she stretched for the mug.

"That service cyborg looks awfully real," I whispered to Theo.

"It can practically do anything a human does," Jem eavesdropped. Suddenly, I had more chills on my arms. She snatched the mug from the wrinkled hands of the cyborg and motioned it to leave.

"Back to where I was," Jem slurped the steamy drink. "World leaders were angered by that woman's speech to keep resolution Pangaea as a temporary solution. The programmers initially set the program for one hundred years, until dismantling into divided nation states. These states would no longer commit war with one-another, as societies around the world would depend on each other's shared history. Unfortunately, her team was eventually forced to make changes to the artificial intelligence, making the program eternal. A handful of world leaders found a secluded location to keep the government's main mother computer secure." Jem looked around suspiciously. I stroked my chin, and the forbidden question rose to mind.

"Do you know where the mother computer with the government is stored?" I asked. The sun reflected on Jem's purple eyeliner.

"Nobody knows, and nobody will know. It might be located on the moon, as far as we can tell from the poor reception," she joked. Theo cracked a giggle, but I remained humorless.

"I know I am a just a military commander, but the computer programmers were right," she added. I leaned back, pretending to not be astonished that this was coming from the mouth of someone with high government authority. "Humans got fed up with a computerized government, and Neo-Revolutionaries would fight and die for their cause of divided human representation."

"So, you-you support the Neo-Revolutionists?" I hesitated. But then again, taking a risk was in my blood. Jem lifted her hand in the air, cutting me short.

"I believe that there must be a dialogue between opposing parties. We are sick of war and need to get to the negotiating table if we will have any chance of lasting peace."

Her dark skin and purple Afro illuminated in the sun. She glanced around the arid room for solitude. Finally, the glimmer in her eyes was gone. She altered the topic of discussion.

"Storm, you are the star in the video feed. You were the only visible person to the millions, including myself watched the devastation that happened Niamey." She continued to glare at me, waiting for me to speak. Theo opened his mouth, almost beginning to spew out his undoubted anger, but I interrupted him before that was possible.

"We are not one hundred percent sure what even happened," I responded. "As far as we know, the military was responsible for almost killing us. There was a nuclear explosion followed by a radiation bomb."

"It was disgusting," Theo added.

"I'm sorry you had to see that. I just want you two to know that it is extremely difficult to be the military commander of the only stable military base in Africa."

"So, who dropped those bombs?" Theo questioned. "Who killed those innocent people with their families at home?" I wrapped my arm around

Theo, preventing him from becoming overwhelmed. Jem frowned, making me feel sympathetic.

"Theo, you are more than welcome to trade shoes with me for a day. You wouldn't survive the series of sacrifices you have to make for the betterment of all."

"Can't you just leave this base if it is so hard for you?" he spewed.

"I have a promotion on the line, and I'm not going to give a damn about what happens to Pangaea once I get it."

"So back to the question," Theo leaned in closer, making my back arch. "Who launched that bomb?"

"I'm sure she said she didn't do it," I said.

"Like I said earlier, military commanders need to make sacrifices…for their promotions," she said, almost too quiet to hear.

My eyebrows moved closer together and so were the pieces of the puzzle. Jem dropped a nuclear and radiation bomb on strongholds for Neo-Revolutionaries and sympathizing civilians. She dropped the bombs to receive her promotion from the digital president. Whatever the promotion was, it must have been worth the possible death of Theo and me.

"You launched that bomb?" I questioned, drifting my grasp off Theo. We locked eyes, understanding the gist of it all. Jem looked at her wristband like it was communicating with her. She seemed like she needed to rush her message.

"Yes, I did, but that is not the topic of discussion. The video feed went offline after both bombs struck, and most citizens in the America province believe both of you are dead," she concluded. My stomach turned at the concept.

"What?" I shook my head.

"Please sit and listen," she said. I stood in protest and Theo followed suit. Blood pumped throughout the veins in my forehead like an elastic bass. I clenched my fist. Jem stood, now taking her time approaching us. Her cold face penetrated the warmth of the room.

"We will give you a public military escort to Chicago so the Americas remain a strong province for us," Jem added. "Chicago may fall very soon, and we need all of the propaganda to make it work." She towered above me and lifted her chin. The mug slanted in her hand, almost spilling the drink onto the soft carpet.

"Why does any of this matter to you?" Theo stepped forward. His trembling tone resonated throughout the silent room. Jem placed her mug on the armrest of the sofa; her back turned against us.

"You are a murderer! You killed thousands of innocent civilians! How do you live with yourself?" Theo cried.

"It is confidential," she said. I almost thought I heard her giggle after she responded.

"How is that so?" Theo barked. I began to place him in restraint. My arm hugged him, feeling his tense muscles contract. Jem held her wrist in her hand, strolling away from us.

"When you go back to Chicago, don't forget to enroll in this month's international health exams." She looked at me distinctively.

"We are feeling better...we just want to go home." I immediately answered, retaining my temperament. She strolled towards the husky, white exit door. The clicks of her boots projected through the soft carpeting.

Bing! The solid door lifted and revealed the entrance to the elevator seating. It was just like the elevator in my apartment building, the seats revealed solid harnesses for the free fall to ground level. She continued to face away from us until she expressionlessly lowered herself on a seat, throwing a harness over herself.

"You would not want to miss these health exams for your lives," she added. With a slam, the elevator door shut our visibility to the unpleasant smirk.

Theo clenched both of his fists. His orange hair covered his right eye, but the left displayed resentment. For a single promotion, no matter how

ample in size, thousands had to be sacrificed. If this
was the world I lived in, I wanted to get out.

CHAPTER
SIX

"Theo, we wouldn't have been in this mess if you didn't bring your stupid video contacts," I said, clucking my lounge, "but it's also my fault for getting us here."

I walked to the reflective window and Theo followed suit. As I surveyed the elevated borders of the military base, I noticed that the sky was abnormally clear. Militarized hovercrafts resembled miniscule ants in the depth below. The black dots scrambled around the base, some shooting into the expanse of the horizon. A blinding sun prevented me from watching the sky. I shifted focus to look at the reflection on the glass. Theo stood beside me, standing stiffer than dead tree bark. He clenched his jaw and held his hands together with a contagious uncertainty.

"We will be home Theo... don't worry about it," I said softly. He shifted his gaze to me.

"She told us to get a health checkup, and I don't know what that was supposed to mean," he shook. "I don't want to die of radiation poisoning." I turned my head. My eyes adjusted to the lighting of the environment. Theo's pale, polished face distinguished itself from the red walls.

"You look fine, Theo." I stepped closer to him, inspecting his dilated eyes and orange hair. His lips puffed. "You're healthy, I promise."

He smiled, exhibiting his well aligned teeth. I kept magnetizing myself closer to him until he unraveled the words.

"Storm, I couldn't have asked for a better friend," he smiled. I gave him a light punch on the shoulder. The silence broke when elevator door swung open with an aged squeal. The open door revealed a young man in a red suit. He brushed his black hair with his hand as he strolled into the conference room.

"Hello! I'm Carter Viel," he said.

"Cyborg or Human?" Theo whispered.

"I really can't tell," I said. The man elegantly held out his hand towards me. It was like he was going to hold something of value.

"I am your escort, and you will be the passengers in my hovercraft," he said. I grasped his hand and shook it firmly. I failed to pinpoint his credentials. His face was flawed and human-like, yet his body language was blocky. Theo grasped his hand and shook it like a feather. He crocked his head to the side as if he held the same question for the escort, but we remained silent to prevent offending the potentially likeable man. His groomed fingernail pointed to the purple suits that hung from the coat hanger. The fashionable suits didn't catch my eye earlier. "Put those on, and we will be on our way."

"What about my hovermobile?" I asked.

"It was automatically sent to Chicago, so let that thought go," he spat. I brought my eyebrows together and shrugged to rebut his authoritative tone. His red suit reflected the hideous attitude.

"Shut up, you hybrid species." Theo blurted. Carter took a step back, holding his hand to his chest. Before I could apologize for Theo's blatancy, he burst into a laugh. He covered his mouth like a well-mannered gentleman form the Victorian age. Theo and I met eyes briefly, reading the odd expression on both of our faces.

"I am a human," Carter composed himself with a grin on his face. "I spent five years in this base alone, so I tend to blend in with the crowd."

"That's very interesting," Theo said with an undertone of sarcasm. I strolled towards the coat hanger to avoid the unusual man. The suits glimmered in the sunlight, and I was hypnotized by its soft cloth. I grabbed the jacket of the purple suit to wrap it around myself. Theo grabbed the pants with the identical suit and jumped into its soft texture. He seemed most intrigued by the designing and material of the clothing, brushing his hand on the soft purple jacket.

"I hope they let us keep these," I said.

"Those are yours to keep," Carter replied.

One leg after another, my magenta pants were wrapped in the suit. The pants automatically tightened to sit comfortably. I glanced below the loose material of the suit to find my naked feet. Theo gestured towards the sparkled dress shoes and socks on the bottom of the coat hanger. I snatched the socks below. If Theo and I wore clothing of higher extravagance than the military commander of the base, our importance gravitated.

I held my chin high as I slipped my sock lathered feet into my shoes. I pulled my shoulders back and strolled into the window's reflection with chutzpah. My confidence flew higher than the structure I stood on. The odd man tapped his foot, patiently lingering for his temporary freedom from the base.

"You must really want to leave this place," I observed.

"I am my family's only support, so I have to do what I have to do," he replied. Theo strolled towards the elevator door, waiting for Carter to lead us to the exit. Carter paced frantically behind Theo. The heavy white elevator door lifted for us. Theo leapt into the corner seat of the elevator and pulled down his harness. I sat beside Theo as Carter scrambled for the seat beside the elevator door. I imagined the help Jem needed to haul our unconscious bodies throughout the tower. I lowered the harness over me and the squeak of the door compressed the elevator.

Immediately, we dropped towards the depth of ground level. I wanted to talk about what we were going to do, but my mind was too caught up in Jem's massacre on Niamey. I was too caught up on the effects on Grandpa's old, frail heart after he assumed I was dead.

As we slowed to a halt, the elevator door cracked open. I was immediately greeted with the gust of warmer air. I lifted the harness and darted outside the clustered space. The sun glared my frail skin, and I looked back. I was never greeted with such sunny weather since my teenage years. Smog always cluttered the beautiful, blue sky. Theo stepped beside me and attempted to look up too.

"Do not do that! You will get blinded!" Carter enlightened. Congested parking zones from military hovercrafts remained perched. It was confusing; why would hundreds of military hovercrafts remain resting on the base's ground when most of Africa was occupied by Neo-Revolutionaries?

"So, where's our ride?" I asked.

"I reserved a special escort," he replied. Heavy engines roared from the distance; it must have been our queue. Three distinguishably colored hovercrafts landed gracefully from the sun. The militarized vehicles were plastered in the Pangaean colors of yellow, pink, and black. Descending to a foot off the solid pavement, I surveyed the yellow and black hovercraft windows, revealing armed guards. I paced towards the empty, pink hovercraft which sandwiched between the security personnel.

"Pink it is," I mumbled. I stepped into the spacious passenger seating. Theo let out an exhausted sigh as he sat beside me. Carter entered through the front of the hovercraft, and he tinkered with the module to shut the doors. Amidst the roaring of the fearless engine, we gracefully lifted to the sun. A gentle acceleration pressed my back lightly against the soft backrest. Thinking about finally arriving home ushered the delight of excitement. I closed my eyes, but before I could indulge in thought, Jem's figure appeared from the holographic display of the center console.

"Storm, Theo, before you enter Chicago, you need to know what you are walking into," she said. *"You will be greeted by media from all throughout the American province and even some spectators. You are both thoroughly responsible for shining the brightest light on Pangaea. I trust you both in doing so."*

"What if we don't?" Theo said.

"Then you'll both be assassinated," she replied. *"Stealth snipers are deployed on almost every sky rise in Chicago. They will shoot on my consent. No Pangaean will*

know who did it. If you both want to live, I insist that you follow the designated plan."

My heart must have skipped a beat. Theo turned to me and whispered.

"I bet she's bluffing."

Despite the possibility, I was more angered by Jem's malevolent character.

"You really disgust me," I sneered. Jem held her sickening grin in the holographic image, continuing without a hiccup of shame.

"Carter has two micro earpieces for you to put on. Once the media ask questions, I will be your tongue," she added. *"Remember to not make it look obvious, stay natural."* I rolled my eyes and looked through the window which displayed the grisly ocean. Carter dug into the pocket of his dazzling red suit, plucking out two micro earpieces. Smaller than a bead, the nude colored earpieces were difficult to take out once they were in the ear. I pinched the micro earpiece and stuffed it in my right ear. Theo appallingly complied with the scheme. Carter seemed to have been the only gratified person on board. He surveyed the windows like a child's visit to an amusement park.

Exhausted, I stretched my legs, slouched on the snug seating, and I decided to shut my eyes. I imagined stealth snipers, subtly crawling around building windows and piercing a bullet in my chest. The thought of Theo and I dying together in a pool of blood sent chills down my spine. I had to distract myself.

"Theo?" I asked with my eyes shut.

"What?" he said.

"What will your parents do when you get home?"

"They'll kill me."

"Please, don't talk about death."

"Jem won't kill us. We're important assets. She just wants another stupid promotion." Theo spoke with his earpiece covered.

"At the cost of human lives," I added. "Let's change subjects." I opened my eyes and scanned Theo's face. "What do you plan to do after this is all settled?"

Theo stroked his thumb on his chin as if he had facial hair.

"I want to get into designing and probably save enough money to move out of Chicago. Maybe I could go to the Mars colony."

"But you told me you wanted to be a journalist in England."

"Yeah well, I changed my mind since Neo-Revolutionaries ran over that place." He jerked his head to the side, flipping his orange hair. "I want to go somewhere far from people. Everything isn't right."

"So, you're sick of me too?"

"No! You're coming with me!" He tugged me to the side, thumping my skull against the window.

"Ow!" I overreacted. I grasped his suit with both hands and pushed him. Theo giggled as the hovercraft rocked from the ruckus.

"Don't do that! We will be thrown off the virtual track!" Carter warned.

"We're not gullible. We know that's not possible." I gestured towards Carter. Theo and I burst into laughter. Carter humorlessly sat in his seat, preventing conflict from the base.

Theo was the partner I always wanted in my life. I knew almost everything about him, and he knew almost everything about me. I could admit that the lust was real, but I silenced it in an irrational fear of rejection. When Grandpa and I moved to Chicago, Theo had to convince his parents to do the same. I was remarkably lucky to find him residing beside me in the same building. Before our arrival in Chicago, Theo and I spent most of our lives in New York City. I couldn't recall the first day we met because we were only five years old. He remembered my chubby cheeks. I also had a heavy lisp which carried throughout fourth grade.

I scanned Theo's dyed hair, reminding me of his passion for manufactured beauty. He had naturally curly brown hair until he decided to shave his head when he was eighteen. It was then that he injected synthetic orange coloring on his scalp. Lasting ten years per dosage, he had had another six years until it became brown again. I was tempted to follow his footsteps, but I loved the organic strands of delicacy on my scalp.

Theo was also an admirer of artificially colored eyes. Every two years, he collected enough credits to visit his eye doctor and inject a new color. From green to blue, to pink, to magenta, to grey, he was always excited about staying on the top of eye color trends. I refrained from his encouragement to correspond our eye colors, but I made up the excuse of loving my natural brown colored eyes. I lied; I was always petrified of needles or anything of that matter getting near my eyes. Also, I was not enthusiastic about wasting hundreds of credits for a simple change in eye pigmentation. Theo knew how to distinguish himself amongst twenty billion people; however, I lacked that unique character. He also has a perfect family with a mother and father. I only had one person of blood in my life: ninety-three-year-old Grandpa.

He told me that my father fled to the Chinese province to start a new life. In doubt, I searched for his name throughout social media sources and public government databases. After hours of endless searching, I failed to find the given name. Grandpa clucked when I showed him the lack of evidence and told me, 'See? He was not even registered in the system. That man was an unlawful fraud!'

When I asked Grandpa about the whereabouts of my mother, all he ever told me was that she died in an accident. Whenever I asked for details of the incident, he would burst into tears, failing to answer. I never asked him more than five times in my life; I felt pity for him. Grandpa was the true definition of a caretaker. He loved my mother, and he was always there when she needed him. I was only three months old when she died in the proclaimed accident. I always wanted to know more, but I stayed humble with what I knew. Grandpa had a simple job as a librarian, and that supplied enough money for a middle-class life. Despite his dry humor and irritating political beliefs, Grandpa always had a silent place in my heart.

Since I was a child, Grandpa reminded me to take care of him on his 'hundredth year,' because every hardworking Pangaean retires when they reach one hundred years of age. I would fulfill that promise for him, especially after all he had done for me. My experiences in the previous few days prove his wisdom was never fabricated.

I wrapped my arm around Theo, the friends I never asked more from, and gazed at the tainted world outside the window. Silently, I thought about the importance of family.

CHAPTER
SEVEN

I felt like my stomach was getting pressed, pushing up the Adrenalin Juice to my mouth. It's a feeling that came when I saw the Tenbrook Tower stand tall on the horizon, homesickness fused with uncertainty. The morning sun caught onto the horizon of Chicago. Thick smog brushed against the windows while the air's bitter taste resituated with my tongue.

"I don't think I'm ready for this." I latched onto Theo.

"Yes, you are," replied the micro earpiece. Jem's distinguishable voice bounced on my eardrum. *"Just don't mess up, and you'll be fine."*
Theo cleared his throat. A droplet of sweat forged on his forehead.

"Good luck, fellas. It was nice meeting you two," Carter said. Recognizable structures darted passed our perception.

Carter targeted for the landing in Millennium Marsh. It used to be a park, but no one has bothered to cut the mutated grass. Flashes of camera drones flustered my sensitive eyes. I was breathing faster than I usually would. Glancing at the crowd below from the secured hovercraft, hundreds of news correspondents rushed towards the strip of greenery.

"You can do this. You can do this," I whispered under my breath. The doors lifted gradually, seeping in the sounds of commotion. It seemed like hundreds were there to see us. Our hovercraft clipped the dead grass. Military personnel from the neighboring hovercrafts stood in two barriers from the exit of the vehicle. Before I could bid Carter farewell, I was pushed out by Theo's forceful tug. I wobbled on my toes as crowds of media reporters rushed towards the resiliently guarded cyborgs. Wind from the active hovermobiles almost pushed me to the dead grass.

"Hurry up. We need to get to the Tenbrook Tower," Theo whispered powerfully, carefully annunciating every word.

"Keep on walking, do not mess up," Jem added. *"Your life depends on it."*

I smiled to the media reporters, the buckling pressure of having my life on the line pushed short lived breaths from my chest. Military personnel created a makeshift circle of isolation around Theo and I. Droned media cameras swiveled around us, making me lose touch with my senses. My heart thumped frantically; my hands moistened in the humidity of the purple suit.

I looked behind for the last time to see the militarized vehicle and I was distantly abbreviated.

Theo kept his gaze low, following my anxious footsteps. The Tenbrook Tower was only four blocks away, but every step was carefully planned, knowing multiple snipers were barbed towards us from the distance. I continued to stage a grin, flapping my hand at the vulture reporters. One reporter broke into the restrained circle. She was professionally dressed in neon colors. Her video drone lowered to capture her report. I gazed at the pavement and paced towards the outskirts of the circle. Before I could shoot a second glance at the woman, her microphone darted towards my direction.

"I have three questions for you, Storm!" the woman shouted. Her raspy voice distinguished itself from the roars of other reporters. "How do you feel now that you have arrived home?"

I gulped and continued to portray my fabricated grin. I waited for Jem's response through the earpiece but failed to pick up a sound. Maybe the signal was out; maybe Jem tested my abilities.

"Do you want me to repeat that question?" she asked. I looked above at the hovering drone. PLL News; this was broadcasting to billions around the globe, yet I failed to produce and answer. Taking initiative, the crack between my lips opened, and I shot out an answer.

"Great! I'm great!" I clamped my moist hands together, waiting for a bullet to pierce my skull. Briefly glancing at the pedestrians watching across the street. The most I could've done was what I gave.

"What did you see in your daring journey to Niamey?" she asked.

"Um." I waited for Jem's response. I sped up my pace but tried to look casual about it. "It was devastating to see the atrocities the Neo-Revolutionaries have caused."

I bit my tongue and lost the grin. Darting my eyes around the city's skyscrapers, I searched for snipers. The Tenbrook Tower's entrance stood several feet away. Reporters with their flashing drones attempted to cram into the circle. I fixated my focus on the approaching doors.

"One last question." The woman placed her hand on the shoulder of my purple suit. I grasped the metal handle of the door, mistakenly planting my feet. "Who do you think dropped the radiation bomb?"

My muscles tensed and I portrayed my best expression of confusion.

"The Neo-Revolutionists did it!" Jem shouted in my earpiece. I opened my mouth, but I was distracted by the odd figure that hung outside the second story of the building across the street. It blended with the building's obsidian color, but its shadow from the morning sun disclosed its character. The mysterious figure barbed something in my direction. I kept watching to notice that it was a sniper.

Theo nudged his hand against my back. I wobbled towards the door's handle, while I attempted to spew the answer. The unnoticeable microphone grasped tightly in the reporter's hand, three inches from my lips.

"Neo-Revolutionists did it," I trembled. I turned away from the smiling reporter and looked indoors the base level of the apartment building. Intrigued residents eyed the glass windows, towards the commotion outdoors. I grasped the metal door handle, relieved. Nobody was shot and no one deserved to be. After this was all settled, I would let the residents know first of what the truth was. Lying about the horrific event in Niamey was shameful, and I was not going to live the rest of my life abiding by that lie.

Despite it, I let out a sigh. I pulled the metal handle on the glass door. Before I could take the first step inside, I jolted from the melody of gunshots.

CHAPTER EIGHT

Shrieks of terror fueled the tainted air, instinctively causing me to duck and lurch for the door. Armed personnel huddled around me amidst the chaos. Theo and I threw ourselves into the immunity of the firm building. He grasped onto me, and we continued to duck from indiscriminate gunfire hitting the bulletproof glass.

"Theo, Are you okay?" I shook.

"I'm okay, are you?" he asked, frowning.

"Yeah," I said. Residents backed from the doors that singled out chaos. Gasps of horror came from those watching. Security personnel formed a barrier outside the entrance and shot several blasts with their weapons onto cloaked targets. Audacious reporters began to disperse from the scene.

"What is this?" I said to the earpiece, feeling my chest tremble, "What did we do wrong, huh?" Amidst the disheveled radio waves, I received a blaring response.

"I'm trying to figure out who must have shot those bullets, just as much as you do; it wasn't me!"

"You are a filthy liar, Jem!" I sneered.

"I don't have any stealth snipers in Chicago! I am the military commander for the Nigerian province and behalf of the African continent, not the Americas, stupid fool!" she replied.

"Tell me who did it before I tell everyone who dropped the bomb!" I choked up a hysterical laugh. Jem tested my maddening limits, but I was willing to disclose anything if I had to. Several residents from the corner of my eye locked their focus on me.

"I swear to you, it was the Neo-Revolutionists! They weren't even aiming for you! You are both unharmed, right? I should have kept silent with you two. I can never trust someone like you."

I froze in my squatted position, scanning the glass doors several feet away. Fractures in the glass of the entryway exhibited itself to the gazing crowd of residents. Clatters continued to pierce the sound of the atmosphere, like crickets. Broad, silver bullets remained frozen in the embrace of the bulletproof glass. Around the fractured glass, stains of blood weaved into the cracks. I lowered my sight to an image I would never forget. Lying lifeless, brushed up against the base of the building, the news reporter's neon green dress glistened in the sunlight. Her black microphone rested several inches away from the tips of her fingers. Bewildered, the video drone sat beside her. My breath halted, and Theo emotionlessly pulled me away from the doors. A lump formed on my neck.

I drew in a breath of whatever energy I held and let out a something between a shout and cry.

I desired to shout out towards the crowds of spectators, but nothing came out. Theo wouldn't stop pulling me away from the entrance. For the first time, I was the irrational one. The doors clicked locked on the imminent lockdown. Lights dimmed in the lobby while the information desk's obsolete robots amplified the programmed procedure.

"Residents, please check-in your apartments and lock the doors. This is a mandatory lockdown."

As I was gasping for air, my eyes moistened, and my lungs compressed. Crowds of residents rushed towards their designated elevators. Mothers paced with their children, students sprinted to their apartments, and others continued to gaze at the horrors outside with apprehension. Theo continued to pull me away from the entrance, and my tensed muscles pushed against his tide. The young reporter didn't deserve it; I did. After several agonizing seconds of Theo taming me from darting outside, I detected a familiar voice, and I stopped.

"Storm," he said. I looked at the hunched figure: Grandpa. He watched me like I was foreign. I shook off Theo's firm grip on my purple suit, leaping into Grandpa's embrace. Tears rolled off my cheeks.

"I-I'm s-so sorry," I wept. Grandpa patted my back.

"It's okay, Storm. It's okay," he replied. I stumbled towards the cluttered congregation of spectators. I wanted to go home, to my real home in New York. Theo silently slipped from the scene. He rushed to his parents who stood unsettled. His mom wiped tears from her eyes as she embraced him. Her orange hair and hollow circles made her look like an impoverished person. Theo's father, like his mother, seemed no different.

"We thought you were dead!" she cried. I closed my eyes, and my shame led me outside the elevator. Before we walked into the doors of asylum, I caught a final glimpse of Theo. He turned his back against me; his parents cuffed his hands with their grasp.

I glided inside the elevator and slumped into the cradle of the seat. Grandpa stood in front of me and lowered a black harness over me.

I made an audacious risk to prove my independence. Today, however, I failed to manage alone. The elevator doors slammed shut, blinding me from the chaos that was resonated through the glass. I let my head lean back and sniffed quietly. I was never the kind to weep, but I learned today that I had the potential to drop tears when it became surreal.

The elevator lifted itself into our designated floor. Motion-sickened squeals resonated from the pulley above. I attempted to clear my thoughts from the graphic image of the lifeless news reporter, but I couldn't shake it off.

We slowed to a halt, and I unlocked the choking harness. I looked at Grandpa with my red, gloomy eyes, but he didn't look back. He kept his gaze down, strolling out the elevator with his wooden walking stick. The aroma of dark chocolate was overridden by the stench of conflict. I stepped into the house I yearned for and absorbed its serenity. The holographic projector was quietly announcing the breaking news.

"Neo-Revolutionists from the Chicago suburbs have advanced into the outskirts of Chicago city. Government officials have called for a mandatory civilian evacuation amid a third attack from the ruthless forces." The third dimensional correspondent gulped. He held his finger to his ear. *"It seems like I'm getting a call that paramilitary and civilian police forces are already making way into the suburbs. This may mean a lack of policing on Chicago streets until the conflict resolves."* I shut my sore eyes and sat on the projector-facing couch.

Grandpa carefully hit the red switch beside the elevator, disconnecting it from potential visitors. I continued to tune-in on the broadcast until I realized my right ear comprehended more than my left. I stuck out my pinky and lodged it into my left ear. Attempting to remove the earbud, Jem's voice irritated my ear canal for a final time.

"Storm, before you take this off, remember to take the health exa-" She was cut short as I plucked out the earbud, chucking it across the room. She was right; the Neo-Revolutionists were a ruthless force. All they ever had was a thirst for blood. Unfortunately, the other side of the malicious coin did the same.

"Storm, we need to talk about something important," Grandpa said. I kept my mouth sealed and challenged my aching eyes to stay wide. Grandpa tapped his walking stick to the ground and he strolled beside me. He puffed out a gust of air as he took a seat. Every day, his puffs only became more severe. I was thinking about it too long, to the point where I was holding my own breath.

I turned towards him, paying attention to the look of guilt on his face. The frown that Grandpa carried should have been gone from the moment he saw me, but he was hiding something more important than that. I recognized the familiar raise of his bushy eyebrows, a scolding I deserved. Grandpa turned to me and held his hands together.

"I wish I told you earlier, but you gave me two lonely days to ponder how I would tell you," he said.

"What is it about?" I said.

"I need to talk about what really happened to your mother." Grandpa let the topic sink into the environment. "I want to tell you before I have to lose you again and maybe never see you again. You're old enough to know now," he added. I raised my eyebrows. "I grew your mother up to be the sweetest woman."

In every conversation about the mother, this was how far Grandpa got before tears rolled down his eyes. I reached out for a box of tissues, but he held out his hand. Despite his rejection, I grabbed a tissue, clearing the corner of my eyes from the tears of terror. Hopefully, they would be the last.

I reminded myself of the medicine that caused Theo and I to fall into a forced coma. The Nano-bots in the capsule would remain embedded in me for a week. They seemed to cure anything: tumors, injuries, depression, and anxiety. It was no wonder I collected myself so quickly. I still wondered where she would receive such valuable medicine, and why she would hand it at no cost.

How did she obtain Adrenalin Juice when all the adrenalin factories were overtaken by Neo-Revolutionaries? Why did Jem want me to get a health checkup so urgently? The pieces of the puzzle were too scrambled for me to comprehend. If it was too complicated to understand, it would be better to not think about it at all.

"Your mother didn't die in an accident." Grandpa's words drifted me back to the topic. I arched my back and laid my head on the headrest of the sofa. Silently, I prayed to any spiritual force to make Grandpa silent. The only thing I wanted to hear from Grandpa was the scolding I deserved. I was only able to ingest so much in one day.

"She had the ambition to foster global peace, and she had a crucial title…Well, that's what it used to be." He placed his thumb on his chin, gazing towards the wall beside me like it was scenery.
"I stood by her every moment of it." Maybe Grandpa fabricated his cries in the past to avoid the truth. I remained quiet to hear the truth seep out of him. "She was working as a secret advisor of the president's social programs, and she reached out to all people. Your mother played a very important role in the world. Defying the president, she initiated peace negotiations with the first Neo-Revolutionist insurgencies. The Virtual Council and President programmed these acts as treasonous, and they sent her to a court for her crimes. She never stopped fighting for awareness of the situation. Right before a judge ordered her execution, she sent a personal letter to all human officials in government to prepare for what was coming. She was right because twenty-one years later, more than half of the world is falling."

Grandpa cleared his throat for the emotional hurdle of the story. "Before she was sent away, she told me-" He sniffed several times and gazed at his hands as he fumbled with them. "She told me to make sure you would continue her fight for peace."

I looked at Grandpa's moist eyes and shook my head. This was something that I should have known before I was able to stand on both feet. Hearing about it now made Grandpa seem like nothing but a stranger.

"Why didn't you tell me this before?" I said.

"I wasn't sure how you would take it. I just wanted you to choose your own path in life, but you needed to know the truth." Grandpa wiped a falling tear from his eye. "I'm sorry I didn't tell you sooner. I couldn't... they were going to send you to a re-education program, but I took custody of you. They told me I had to change my identity, and I would face execution if you knew the truth." I observed his real tears; the tears of agony. I placed my fingers on the temples of my head and rubbed.

I held myself in the same position until Grandpa understood I needed to be left alone. Second, after second, I felt the stress build up like a frail dam with too many cracks. After roughly two minutes, Grandpa picked himself up and let his walking stick guide him to his room. The clicks of the stick pounded much slower than the rhythm of my heart. I finally broke the silence that I held for too long.

"Grandpa," I said. He turned around to hear me speak. "It's okay."

He brought his lips together, bringing the edge of them slightly upward; a sincere smile. He continued to his isolated room. Before his door closed, I stood up and paced into my bedroom. The heat of the dark walls was choking me alive. I grabbed the blue plush pillow from my bed, pressing it against my face. As loud as I could, I screamed into its suffocating layers. I took the foolhardy risk to visit Niamey, witness the atrocity, get drugged, and have an innocent news reporter killed, all because of me.

The sniper should have shot me instead, but I had the privilege to continue living the experience. I know what killed my mother, and I wanted revenge for all of those who indoctrinated me to love this filthy world. I took a deep breath, getting tamed by the medicine inside me. Maybe it was time to isolate from the world. I could remain sealed in for an extensive period. My room had a refrigerator, a balcony, and mirror to talk to.

It did not concern me if the situation took days, weeks, or even months to settle. I was not going to step outside until my pseudo-popularity subdued. As I lobbed the blue pillow onto my bed, I heard a familiar jingle from the mirror. I launched myself towards the words on its screen.

Theo is calling. Pick up? The reflection displayed dark circles and hair that grew in the wrong direction; I was already a shell, alive inside, dead out. My purple suit seemed far from worn. The edges toned my weak shoulders. Maybe that was why all government officials wore suits. It was because they were frail and weak inside its deceiving look.

"Yes," I said. Theo immediately appeared on the other side of the mirror. His long face seemed more worried than sorrowful. The vibrant suit was gone, replaced with colorless sleepwear. Despite it, he still seemed handsome. I could have only wished that I did not look like a walking corpse, traumatized and stuck in a hideous cycle of restlessness.

"Hey, Storm," he said.

"What do you want?" I said.

"Are you sure you're okay? I don't want to lose you to anything stupid," he added. I wobbled my head and stepped closer to the mirror.

"I don't want to see anyone here." I began to shake. "I'm sick of everything, and all I want is for this whole situation to die dow-"

"It won't, Storm," he interrupted. He replicated my signature squint and darted his eyes at mine. "I've been twitching a little, and I'm worried that there was something in those pills."

"Can't you wait it out?" I asked. Theo paused for two seconds, glancing around his mirror for a feasible answer.

"We need to get our health checkups sooner than later. Even Jem told us to do it," he replied.

"Do you believe a thing Jem told us?"

"No, that's exactly why we need to get checked up. Heck, we don't even know what kind of drug she dosed with."

"Theo, if we step outside, we could end up like that reporter! How do you think we will slip by? Disguise ourselves?" I knew I would receive an abbreviated response from the look on his face. He smirked, the kind of smirk he gives when he thinks of something clever.

"Yeah."

"You're simply anxious. I am too, but you need to ignore your twitching."

"I don't care if I'm being insane. I need to know what is happening with me, and you're coming with me whether you like it or not, Storm."
Theo was particularly assertive as if the trauma triggered him to numb all his emotions, explicitly fear. He was never this impudent on a regular day, but it seemed like he knew exactly what to do to when survival was the forefront of his mindset.

"When do you want to go?" I asked quietly. He casually glanced around for an answer and raised his navy-blue eyebrows.

"The best time to sneak out is seven o'clock. I hope the building's lockdown will be over by then. Everyone is too scared, hiding up inside. We can get our blood checked for anything that she gave us."

"I'm telling you, Theo. You're just anxious about nothing." I paused to read the words in his eyes, hardly open. "But I'm only doing this because I got you into this mess in the first place."

"How will we sneak out without getting targeted by who knows what?" he asked.

"We will need a good cover... I can't really think of one right now," I added. Suddenly, Theo lifted his finger in the air as if it were a breakthrough.

"Drug addicts," his eyebrows were raised.

"What?"

"We will dress up as drug addicts and sneak out of here in a jiffy."

"I'm not sure if I can pull that off."

"Remember, today at seven," he said. Before I could refute, Theo faded from the mirror, revealing my tiresome character. I stepped near the entrance to the balcony, letting my hand grasp the thick curtain. I pulled it to the side to catch a glimpse of several news broadcasting drones hovering the dull streets. If only those media drones were in Niamey to capture the blasts, I wouldn't need to lie through my teeth.

Smog blanketed the view of the streets and the depths of the city. The sun glared against my window like a spotlight. A vast array of questions had to be answered, and only Theo and I held the answers in a locked down building. Thousands of daredevils were there in Niamey, yet none had the footage we had.

Theo and I would be more valuable dead knowing such information.

Despite it, it was time to act. A lifeless tomato plant perched in the corner of the room. Dry dirt under the stale plant was a memorabilia of my week's old inadequacy to care for any plant. The concept was forming into place. I swiped a pair of rusty scissors from beneath the bed. I cut the fabric of air several times. It was game time.

CHAPTER
NINE

A pair of black, unwashed sweatpants with several strains of pizza sauce and flour drooped from the abandoned corner of the closet. I tried to make something delicious on the first day in this apartment, but of course, nothing transpires in my vision.

I reached out to grab the pants and throw them towards the nearly deceased tomato plant. It flattened the dirt, the spine of the plant collapsing. I scanned the array of hoodies that hung in a consecutive channel, wrapped around metal hangers. Next to the hoodies laid a pile of tank tops. Chicago had unpredictable weather, which was true from the moment I stepped into the city. It would be sweltering hot in the morning and snow by night. I never understood how native Chicagoans dealt with such fluctuation.

Selecting the littlest of all evils, I chose the hoodie that Grandpa gifted me on my nineteenth birthday. The mossy sweater with thick fabric was a pricey piece of clothing, but I never dared to put it on. I raised my rusty, squeaky clippers towards the hideous sweater. Clip after clip, I began to wound the fabric.

The sweater hurdled towards the pot of dirt when I was done.

I didn't want to finish the job. My eyes were reeling shut. Maybe Theo was right; something about the medicine she gave us remained embedded in our system. I was always feeling tired, but that could have been the uncertainty whispering. I dropped the shears in the closet and dropped myself onto the bed. I backed into the embrace of the plush bedding and flattened into the elasticity of the mattress. The sole of my right foot lightly clipped a sharp object. I winced, examining what stubbed my heel. The wooden box was an old makeup kit, something I forgot stuffing under my bed. I snatched the box and moved to the mirror. I slumped onto the seat facing it, and I laid the box on my lap.

Click! Click! Squeaking hinges revealed the vast array of concealers and eye shadows. I was anticipated to begin my altercation, but I let out a gust of ashamed wind. Men should be proficient in applying all kinds of makeup on themselves. Theo was sharp in his styling and colors, but I lacked the fine knowledge in this craft.

I snatched a lighter color. I dabbed the brush into the concealed, diligently. My mind visualized the previous time Theo applied makeup on himself. I drove the tip of the dark concealer an inch under my eye. Stroke after stroke, the cool tip lathered the misty tone under my eyes. I already had a pair of natural droops under my tiresome eyes, but the light concealer fashioned a severe appearance of malnutrition, something very odd today.

Tilting my head in several directions, I approved my attempt in the arts. I stood from the seat and made a second attempt to rest on the plush bed. My back fell into the embrace of the cold comforter. The harmony of wind brushing against the window persuaded me to rest. I shut my tiresome eyes. After several short minutes, I drifted into a long-awaited nap.

"You are receiving a call from Theo. Would you like to answer this video call?" The mirror awakened me. The windows were dark, disclosing the night sky. I leaned in towards the mirror.

"Answer it," I groaned. The mirror illuminated its screen, revealing an unrecognizable individual. I rubbed my eyes to clear the haze. A bright light caused me to squint. Theo was wearing torn black clothing; he tailored the scuffed shirt with breathtaking deterioration. The jeans torn and patched, representing a fashion trend of the twentieth century.

"It's almost seven, Storm! Wake up!" He inched closer to his mirror. A yawn rushed forward. Although time traveled with grace in my world, it seemed like the opposite with Theo. I found my feet and placed them on the floor. My eyes yearned to keep shut. I didn't bother to respond to the frantic waves on the screen. I swayed in several directions before leaping from the bed.

"I'm getting ready," I mumbled. My body magnetized to the bedding; I was beyond drained from his interruption. "Is the building still on lockdown?"

"No, the doors opened two hours ago. You missed the people running out with their luggage. The neighbors that stayed called me a few minutes ago. They told me about strangers camping outside our elevators, maybe waiting for us to take a flight downstairs.

"They know where we live?" I shook awake.

"Those rusty, crappy cyborgs sitting by the information desk say anything to anyone who asks." Theo shook his head. I rushed towards the mucky clothing on the soiled pot. Unearthing scoops of dirt with my bear hands, I rubbed the dry compos onto the hoodie and sweatpants. Afterwards, I rushed towards the mirror with the clothes in hand.

"How does this look," I said, exhibiting the clothes in both hands to the mirror.

"That looks perfect!" he said. "Now, wear it."

I stepped aside from the mirror, stripping from the purple suit and patriotic pants. I walked to the closet and snatched the portable shower bottle. I shot its chilling antibacterial mist all over my bare body. I hopped into my sweatpants and tossed on the ripped hoodie.

"Okay, I will be down soon," I said, walking back towards the mirror.

"Wait, Storm. How are we going to get down there without the elevators?"

"It seems like the only option available to us is the stairs," I said.

"I guess that's the plan then," he said, disconnecting the call. I was once more forsaken by the image of my reflection. The unnerving image made me wince. I tiptoed towards the door in the darkened room and remained vigilant of Grandpa. The door lifted to an eerie, darkened living room. Grandpa's room remained shut. I advanced towards the emergency staircase beside the elevator. The unused metal door projected it squeal across the apartment unit.

"Shut up," I whispered to the lifeless door. I silently entered the cluttered stairwell. Lights remained dimmed, and stairs unveiled patches of rust. My hand gradually choked the door's passageway until I heard a click.

I prepared myself for the tedious walk with a long sigh. I threw on my hood and kept my gaze low. Step after step; flight after flight, I had to make my way across one hundred and thirty-two flights of stairs.

CHAPTER TEN

"Ouch!" I groaned, slipping for the third time in the descent. I lunged forward but caught my grasp on the rusty railing beside me. My back was hunched, and my lips remained apart to gasp for the thick air. Sweat trickled down my polished body. Wounds in my hoodie prevented my skin from suffocating as the wind passed through its cracks.

All sweatpants could do was sponge the sweat. I maintained an alert ear for footsteps ahead or below me. Despite detecting the melody of leaking water pipes, the building was relatively lifeless. I jerked my head up towards the rusty sign in the stairwell.

Floor two. A grin plastered on my face. I released the assisting metal railing. A manual door halted me in my tracks. Despite it blocking my way, I continued to limp forward until my body slammed against the miniscule window planted on the door.

Ground level: a five second elevator fall was limited to a laboring thirty minutes. I looked around for clearance. The empty lobby conducted a chill throughout my spine. I've never seen it this quiet and lifeless.

I approached the help desk of the lobby, but the corner of my eye caught the glimpse of several men guarding my elevator door. Black suits and tinted sunglasses, they stood intimidatingly in place, scanning around the empty lobby for their wanted suspect. I continued limp to prevent the unveiling of my identity.

Tap! Tap! Tap! Boisterous footsteps from the corner of my senses caught up to several feet behind me. I caught small pockets of air, my shaking arms were out to push out the next door. Before I slid through the cracks of the exit, I mistakenly turned my head around. A bulky man in a black suit, sunglasses, and dress shoes held out his hand, motioning for me to halt.

"Stop right there!" he said. I threw open the exit door and leaped out of the indoor premises. My chest jumped past my feet. Cool winds splashed onto my face, trickling onto every inch of exposed skin. Theo stood alongside the building, laying his weight on the wall. He seemed so worriless.

"I live ten stories above you," he said, "how long does it take yo-"

"Theo, run now!" I shrieked. He let go of his relaxed pose as he glanced over at the suited man's sprint. I passed Theo, but he was quick to catch up. As we approached the end of the block, I was distracted by the lack of traffic, police, and sources of a sanctuary.

"Help!" My voice cracked.

"Over there!" he said, pointing towards the dim lit medical building two blocks away.

I glanced over my shoulder to the several men, running like lions on prey. I needed to run faster, but my legs were too exhausted for wide strides. I felt the adrenalin kicking in, narrowing my vision and squeezing every muscle in my body. One of the men held his hand out to leap and tackle. We crossed the crumbling street without daring to look on either side. Fragments of concrete crumbled under the weight of my boots.

"Help!" I shouted again. My pleas cramped my abdomen. Several hundred feet from the medical building, Theo leaped through the second row of streets. I glanced over my shoulder one last time to see an empty sidewalk.

"They're gone," I slowed my pace. My lungs struggled to capture the piercing cold air, but Theo threw himself towards the entrance, lurching open the door.

"Get in!" he roared. I leaped into the building, scanning for life. Several policed cyborgs pointed their weapons towards us. Their faces were covered in black masks, an attempt to strike fear in those that attempted to challenge them. I raised my hands in the air.

"Can you help us? We were just being chased by these men." I pleaded. One cyborg officer stepped up, continuing to barb his heavy weapon.

"No, we can't assist you," it said.

"What? But we were almost killed! We need your hel-"

"This city is in a state of emergency. All police are patrolling for rebel activity in the suburbs. We are only guarding government buildings in the city center."

I placed my hand on Theo's shoulder, leaning on him. Theo watched the doctor unassumingly sitting behind the metal desks. He was grey-haired like my history professor. Headphones were jabbed in his ears. Maybe he was unaware of the two patients ahead of him.

"We want a monthly health checkup." Theo hesitated to the trigger holding officers. Simultaneously lowering their weapons, the masked police stepped aside to their defensive stance. Theo led me towards the desk that held an inattentive doctor. My throat whistled, inhaling and exhaling the tainted air. Theo held his firm physique. The doctor in white jumped from his seat.

"Look, I don't want any problems, okay?" he said, unplugging his headphones.

"This is just a costume to get by," Theo said. The doctor smiled and reached for his notepad. I was appalled by the doctor's negative reaction to our costumes but not the conflict in Chicago which caused anarchy on the streets.

"Come with me," he insisted. His grey hair spelled experience, yet his youthful tone of voice disclosed a hair dye. He led the way into the emergency room nearby.

"But this isn't an emergency." I let loose a forced laugh.

"Nobody is as crazy to even step out of their homes," he replied. "You're the only people here."

"What happened?" I blurted. "I'm sorry, I was asleep, and I woke up to this madness"

"Chicago's suburbs are falling to Neo-Revolutionists, young man," the doctor said. "If I were you, I would make something out of your life and move out before the city is occupied." He scanned once more at our impoverished look, almost believing that it was our authentic representation. A pessimistic expression came from him throughout the entire procedure. He pricked our fingers, evaluated our health status, and he held the same look while we returned to the desk.

"Well, as far as I can tell, you are both extremely healthy. Good for you…it's off the charts," he said.

"What does that mean?" Theo asked.

"Your expected life expectancy is one hundred and fifty years if you continue your current route."

"I was twitching earlier," Theo said. "I was scared it must have been a side effect from the..."

I tugged Theo with my foot before he mentioned any lavish medicine. As far as I could tell, Jem handed something that wasn't approved by any health institution.

"It's nothing to worry about," the doctor concluded. "As for your results, I will submit them to the database."

"I'm glad to hear that," Theo let go a sigh of relief. I was swift to intervene.

"So, how will you put these results in the database if you don't know our names?" I said. The doctor stood and strolled around the desk. He placed his hand on my shoulder while our eyes met.

"Theo, Storm, you two must work on disguising yourselves better. I believe that is why those men chased you. As for your safety, I'll spare you a police cyborg. It's not like this hopeless clinic needs ten anyways. It will only escort you to your building." He gestured to one of the guarding officers, and it stepped up behind us.

"Thank you very much, sir," I replied with grinning heart.

"I am the only doctor here, and I will stay as long as this fragile building does," he said. Before he strolled behind his designated desk, he concluded with his farewell. "For Pangaea!"

"For Pangaea," Theo replied with lifeless pride. Following from behind, the officer guided us to the main street.

"I told you it was nothing to worry about," I growled. "Look at what we got into."

Theo glanced at me and then looked expressionlessly ahead.

"Well, we aren't hurt," he said. I pointed to my bruised knee.

"You don't understand what it's like to go down those stairs."

We crossed two blocks with relative silence. I could have detected two hovermobiles fly above us, but that was as busy as it got.

As we entered the silent building, the silent cyborg swiveled back to its place of origin. I observed my designated elevator, seeing no signs of life. The lobby was empty, but we tip-toed through the marble flooring. Information cyborgs sat in their designated positions, smiling at the both of us. Every Cyborg has the tendency to make me feel uneasy, especially when they're forcing emotions that I need least. I latched onto Theo's arm while we entered the stairwell.

"You're not running ahead of me," I reminded the athletic figure. He rolled his eyes and hunched his back. I grinned with an undertone of retribution as we I hiked back up the staircases.

Unfortunately, gravity added the pinch.
All that came to mind was the "off the charts" health results. It didn't sound right, but it was too late to put it under questioning. Theo and I spent our entire lives inhaling tainted air, consuming junk food, and hardly moving a muscle when need be.

"Jem kept on stressing this checkup," I commented. Theo remained silent, maybe pondering the idea himself. Like a riddle, I needed to think abstract if I wanted to find an answer.

CHAPTER
ELEVEN

I stayed up all night, looking through the thick window to my balcony. I couldn't sleep, but maybe that was because I decided to take a nap earlier. The glistening lights from the windows of structures that once illuminated the skyline gradually began to dim. Once the smog cleared from lifeless factories, I witnessed late asylum seekers and their families leave the scene. The atmosphere itself was deceased. It seemed like only the sympathizers of Neo-Revolutionaries remained in their homes. Open windows from across the street exhibited parties. After the sun peeked from the lake, I could hear violent bombardment. Like Niamey, the suburbs fell into the abyss and the city followed suit. Civility transformed into chaos on such short notice.

Several militarized hovercrafts cluttered the brown skies. Twenty minutes from sunrise, I watched the centuries old Willis Tower which was only several blocks away. Indistinguishable and unrecognizable characters unhooked the Pangaean flag from the building's tip. The team of Neo-Revolutionaries lobbed the pink, yellow, and black flag onto the eerie streets. Immediately after dropping it, they holstered a flag of a hardly recognizable design with red and white stripes. A blue square on the upper left corner of the flag displayed an organized congregation of white stars.

"Can you give me a news update?" I asked the mirror.

"I'm sorry Storm, there is no connection. Please try again later," replied the mirror.

The Pangaean government had already cut internet access to Chicagoans. With nothing else to do, I looked at the clock that hung on my bedroom wall; digits read six in the morning. Waiting for Grandpa was like waiting for the dentist. It was time to wake him up. I made my way to his bedroom door.

Knock! Knock! Knock!

"Grandpa?" I silently waited for a reply. "Grandpa, are you there?"

After lingering for a minute outside his room, anxiety gradually crept into me. My heartbeat throbbed faster with every passing second and thought. He was in his room for almost fourteen hours, and he was silent for the entire time. I pounded on the metal door for a response. The palm of my hand anguished with every thump.

"Grandpa, open up now please!" My head rushed with the possibilities of his condition. He was too old to be left alone in a locked room. Before I could bruise my hand with another round of thrashing, I heard a scuffle from the other side of the door. The door slid up to let me exhale relief. Grandpa tiresomely stood at the other side of the door. His flashy, grey nightwear clung tightly to his frail body.

"What happened?" he said, sensing urgency.

"I thought something happened to you. You were in that room for hours," I said.

"I was writing letters to old friends."

"Why?" I peeked my head past him, looking at the wooden desk with handwritten letters scattered around. Grandpa was the only person I knew that handwrote letters. I aspired to have a skill in handwriting, but my hand trembled too much with the grasp of a pen. Besides, I would rather type than swivel my hand around in shaky scribbles.

"Because I'm bidding them a farewell," he said. "We need to get out of here like everyone else."

"Are you sure?" I attempted to scan his honesty. "I thought you would want to stay here with your community."

"You saw what happened in Niamey. The Pangaean military will round up all the loyalists for evacuation and kill what is left, including revolutionary sympathizers."

"I'm not sure if they would do that to Chicago," I said. "There's still a chance that the military can win, and we can stay safe."

"There is no such thing as safe. We have to pack and leave before noon hits the sky."

"Leave where?" I questioned. Grandpa strolled to his desk, folding the illustrated papers. He ignored my question, but I was aware that he had to ponder it thoughtfully. I walked back to my room and returned to my post beside the balcony window, sitting and waiting. We stayed in Chicago for what was hardly a week, and it was already over. I could have called it the worst vacation.

Before I stood to pack my belongings, flashes captivated me towards the window. A delivery drone headed towards the balcony's direction; a tiny, yellow package dangled below the clamp. The drone buzzed its four propellers over the balcony and unlatched the enveloped sized package onto the dusty floor. The drone left back to its place of origin. The miniscule package remained still, waiting to be picked.

I was not able to imagine anyone sending a letter sized message. Maybe, just maybe, it was for Grandpa. However, I wanted to know what was in it. I held my breath and slid open the balcony door. I was greeted with the dust of warm, tainted air. Smog seeped beside me, latching onto the fabric in my bedroom. My hand picked the light package, and I threw myself into the sanctuary. I hauled the door close, and I let in a deep breath of filtered air.

Curiosity rattled the yellow package; it seemed vacant from the inside. I ripped open the thin layering of covering, exposing a cardboard box. As I dug into it, a slip of paper fell from the empty package. I clutched the small piece of paper that landed face down on the floor. Plastered in the middle of the small paper, a colorful stamp in the colors of yellow, magenta, and obsidian black legitimized its source; the Pangaean government. Flipping it revealed the handwritten words:

Congratulation, Storm Raleston. Your proficient health score from the database has elected you a mandatory position on Mission Alpha Centauri. Please report to the Capital Space Station in New York as soon as you can with all your belongings. I will explain the credentials once you arrive. If you do not check-in at the space station by 12 pm CT, you will face felony charges.

Sincerely, Jem Hata

I flipped the note once more. Capital Space Station: the largest Space Station in the world. It was situated in my home city. I repetitively glanced over the letter until my eyes ached.

Mission. Felony. Jem. The health checkup landed me here, giving me no option at all. Thanks to Theo, I was caught in the grasp of it.

"Grandpa!" I shouted.

113

"What?" he asked.

"You need to come here and see this."

He clacked his walking stick against the floor, making his way to my bedroom. I held the letter towards him. My hand was shaking, but that was because I was thinking of a plan to sneak from this subscription. Grandpa scanned the white letter, gradually dropping his jaw. He snatched the paper from my hand and flipped it to view the stamp. I was taken back from him. He wasn't acting like himself.

"This can't be!" He dropped his walking stick and wrapped his arms around me. I stepped back, shaking my head.

"What is this?" I asked. He loosened his grasp, thoroughly scanning the paper for the second time.

"Project, rather Mission, Alpha Centauri was a project your mother worked decades for." He continued to cement a smile of pride on his aged face.

"What does this mean?" I spoke faster than I thought. Grandpa silently walked over to the balcony window and watched the sky. His mouth discarded the grin, and his shoulders swayed.

"It doesn't mean anything good," he said.

"Tell me, Grand-"

"We need to pack. We're going to New York," he said, limping to his bedroom. Before I could break the silence, he turned to me. "Take a real shower, and change out of that horrendous clothing."

From there, he disappeared into his room. I was not sure if he was energized by anxiety or excitement. I stood beside my closet, yanking a favorite pair of clothing from the metal hangers: blue jeans with a blue sweater. I rested the clothing on my shoulder and picked a pair of leather boots. I walked to the bathroom, and the automatic, hefty door lifted for access.

I threw myself into the marble-walled bathroom. The door behind me shut close. I looked at my reflection in the bathroom mirror. My eye shadow and concealer were notably smeared. I dropped my foul clothes in a pile. I walked myself into the shower. The ceiling was littered with hundreds of water shoots.

"What type of shower would you like?" the artificial intelligence asked, embedded in the ceiling of the bathroom. I pondered the choices.

"I want a heavy thunderstorm with roughly warm water," I replied. Suddenly, the relaxing roars of thunder engulfed the bathroom. Lukewarm water from the shoots trickled on my skin. For several serene minutes, I closed my eyes and savored it all. The detachment from reality was a detachment I yearned for. I never disliked showers; I simply lacked the time to take one. Maybe I needed to take more showers in my free time, rather than occupy myself with unnecessary tasks.

"Please state your desired fragrance," it asked.

"I want to smell like mint," I replied. A mist of minty soap drizzled from the ceiling. I rubbed my scalp, removing the grime from days of collected moisture. Tranquil thunders in the bathroom coincided with the thumps on the metal door. My lungs let out an irritated groan.

"What?" I shouted.

"Hurry up, Storm!" Grandpa replied.

"Okay, Okay!" I rubbed my face, removing residue makeup. "Shower, dry me."

The droplets of minty cleanliness, alongside the cracks of thunder, halted. Tiles on the walls of the shower broke open, revealing blow-drying vents. They began to whine, pushing temperate winds to my moist skin. The winds hardly dried every crevice of my body. I stepped out of the shower prematurely.

I cloaked my skin in the clean outfit, captivated by my reflection. I was finally myself again. I brushed my hygienic, glossy hair to a side with my hand. The aroma of mint radiated from my skin. I stepped beside the door, and it lifted to the view of several filled plastic bags. Cool air whisked by my clean skin, inducing me to shiver. Grandpa struggled to haul the bags into the living room.

"What are you doing?" I asked. Grandpa glanced at me and puffed.

"I packed for you," he said.

"I'm sure we have plenty of time to make way to the station. What's the rush, Grandpa?"

"I do not want you to miss it…you cannot miss it."

"I will be there on time. Don't worry." I stepped into the cool living room, wrapping my arms around myself. "Did you pack everything?"

"I packed all of your clothing, your gadgets, and hygienic products."

All that remained was my bedding and mirror. Questions rose to mind, but one lingered on my tongue. I had to spit it out.

"We aren't coming back, are we?" I said. Grandpa walked to the elevator's connection panel that was embedded in the wall and hit the switch for reconnection. His hands trembled with uncertainty.

"I can't make any promises," he answered. I already knew that it meant we were never coming back. Whenever Grandpa failed to make a promise to me, it simply meant that 'it' was not going to transpire. My hands silently hauled the four plastic bags, and I made way into the elevator. I carefully locked each bag into a seat. I sat and locked myself in a harness; Grandpa followed suit. I was okay with the idea of never coming back. Chicago was worse than anything I have imagined. New York was where I belonged.

"What about your luggage?" I questioned.

"Don't worry about it, Storm. It will stay here with your mirror and bed," he replied.

It was almost unsettling. I was leaving but Grandpa was not? Why was that so? Maybe it was because I was put up for a military conscription. Grandpa wouldn't have been so thrilled if that was the case. Whatever it was, he was never a fan of questions. He'd rather leave me in the dark, and in the dark, I remained.

The elevator shut its doors. I had a final glimpse of the living room. It wouldn't be missed. The black plastic bags trembled in their fastened harnesses on the drop to ground level. A squeaky elevator door revealed a silent lobby. I pulled the bags from the unlocked harnesses, pacing faster than Grandpa towards the exit. My leather shoes echoed with every click. The bullet riddled, glass exit doors sent chills down my spine. My legs kicked the plastic bags stuffed with clothing. I walked into the eerie parking lot. Ten hovermobiles remained parked, including mine. My shoulders slouched as I struggled to haul the bulky bags.

I tapped my wrist to unlock the clunker doors. I felt my finger brush against my wrist. My dilated pupils frantically aimed wrist to wrist. It must have fallen into the bathroom shower. Grandpa unlocked the hovermobile doors with his wristband. He observed my cluelessness and prevented me from making any rash decision.

"Don't worry, Storm. You will get a new one," he said.

I threw my bags into the back seats and slouched onto the passenger seating. Grandpa dropped himself in the driver seating and let out his signature sigh.

Operation Alpha Centauri, the letter said. I never heard of such recruitment in my life. Grandpa set in the coordinates and initiated flight for the space station. Before the hovercraft darted into the familiarly hollow virtual path, before the lengthy flight of warzone detours, and before I hushed myself in the imprisonment of the cabin, I took a glimpse of the Tenbrook tower. I didn't know that it was the last place I called home.

CHAPTER TWELVE

"Grandpa, can you please spill the beans?" I asked. Grandpa continued to gaze at the virtual path ahead, giving my question no attention. Towers on the horizon stroked the grey sky of New York City. Although it was miles away, I could smell the streets from the cabin. Hovermobiles lined up in the sky as they reached their asylum.

"Ah, look, we are here!" he declared. I surveyed the hundreds of white launch pads that littered the once green lands. Bulky borders around the space station reminded me of Jem's military base. Lavish space shuttles with decorative styling scattered around the base. The wealthy and their decorative space shuttles had first class access to the Mars and Moon colonies. I only wished to become wealthy to leave Earth.

Suddenly, I locked my gaze to three enormous spaceships. Plastered in the colors of yellow, pink, and black, the structured masses were the largest I had ever witnessed. Thousands of circular windows blanketed the walls of the spaceships. They were erected taller and wider than the Tenbrook tower.

"Grandpa, look at those!" I pointed my finger. Grandpa turned his head to the spectacle.

"That's where you're going!" he said, but he was quick to blanket his voice.

"What?" I shook my head. He must have been joking, because I had never visited space in my life, and thought I never would. Most people visited space before they became an adult. I was the exception, all because I was poorer growing up. While the hovermobile glided to a landing in the parking lot, I unbuckled my harness. "Okay, tell me what is going on," I added.

Ignoring my lightheartedness, he continued to direct the conversation in another direction.

"So many launches happen here, the dirt has turned to sand," he said. "It is crazy to thi-"

"Stop! Tell me what is going on!" I demanded. While the neon pink hovermobile caressed the cemented parking lot, he stuck out his frail hand towards me and patted my back. His eyes looked at the windows but failed to lock onto me. The wrinkles on his forehead intensified. "I'm getting sent out, am I?"

"Storm, this is extremely important," he said.

"This looks like a very expensive vacation to me." I pointed my hand towards the towering spaceships.

"You will be sent into space with many people that are just like you to make new friends."

"Is this a military mission?"

"No."

"So, when will I come back?"

Grandpa looked at me; his eyes were glossy. I gulped the uneasy breeze. He grasped my shoulder tighter than before. I felt the tremble in his restless hand, perpetuating my leg to flutter with anxiety. Goose bumps formed on my pale forearms.

"You don't," he replied, stuttering. Suddenly, my lungs dropped to my stomach, failing to catch a breath. The walls of the cabin squeezed. I flung open the door, stepping outside. Humidity continued to choke my hazed perception.

"No, you can't do this to me!" I barked. Grandpa gently stepped onto the cement parking lot. His eyes remained frozen concealing whatever emotion he had.

"Storm, this is the best for you," he said. I paced away from Grandpa, towards the skyline that glistened in the distance. New York seemed beautiful from this angle, mostly underappreciated. I left friends, acquaintances, and most importantly, memories in the boundaries of the city. Sand littered the lightly traced road. The thought of running from the space station caught me. I could temporarily seek refuge and buy time for Grandpa to rethink his rash decision.

"They will find you," he said, strolling to the closed gates of the station. "This time, they won't miss their target."

Grandpa struggled to carry the several plastic bags. He knew I would follow him. After all, his wisdom was far from fabricated. I had to force myself to a decision, and so I dragged behind his lead. We stepped closer to the gates and they began to crack wide enough for his entrance.

"You can't do this to me." I looked at him, but our eyes didn't meet. The deafening clack of the gates throbbed against my eardrums. Hundreds of space shuttles cluttered the view of the tainted sky like a skyline itself.

Suddenly, a figure from the distance stepped into expanding the picture of the interior of the space station. The signature crooked smile resonated from her face. Jem held out her hand to me, but I had no other choice than compliance.

"I am so glad you were able to come," she said, shaking my hand. "You will not regret this life-changing decision. I promise."

A sense of security slipped from her purple lipstick. Priority blanketed her expressions. I pursued to grin back at her but had too much to ask in the short notice.

"I have so many-" I said.

"Questions, right?" Jem replied. I quivered from her sharp response. "Don't worry... I will deliver all of the details once I give you a brief overview of this mission." Jem's voice muffled amidst the sounds of closing gates. I watched the towering yellow, magenta, and black spaceships half a mile away.

I felt like I was cornered. There was no way out of this. My knees dropped to the pavement, and I winced.

"I don't want to do this, please!" I cried.

"It's too late now. You're already here." Jem waved her hand up, almost in disappointment.

"Get up, Storm," Grandpa insisted. He dropped the bags onto the pavement, reaching towards me. The blue veins in his hand contrasted with his pale skin. I shook my head, remaining planted on the floor. I did not know how to respond to the overwhelming reality other than to perch on the ground. Jem sighed and sat on the ground next to me. Her pink skirt stuck to her thigh as her purple boots creaked.

"You do not know how lucky you are, Storm," she said.

"How am I lucky? I am being sent out to never come back." I said, not certain if my eyes moistened from the overwhelming pressure or the humid atmosphere. Jem looked at Grandpa and back at me, lowering her voice.

"Pangaea is bound to be overthrown. Neo-Revolutionaries are overrunning every city, and they have now acquired nuclear ballistic missiles. Storm, this is a nuclear war. Many analysts predict that most, if not all of Earth's population would be wiped out in the upcoming fight."

"No, that can't be," I denied. I choked on the humid air, tears seeped from my eyes. My hand cleared the traces of vulnerability. "You need to warn people."

"Nobody listens to the government anymore, Storm," she said. "The only loyalists that remain on this blasted planet are the ones that have fled to New York City."

I attempted to speak but failed to think of anything to say. Like a leaf in a breeze, I felt like I had no control over my fate. Looking at the massive, color coded spaceships turned my stomach. Jem struggled to stand up. She motioned to her police cyborgs to carry my baggage.

"Place this luggage under the name of Storm Raleston," she informed. Before she walked into the depths of the space station, the gates cracked open once more. I rose to my feet. A gust of heat brushed on me from the venting gates. An energetic, orange-haired character threw himself through the cracks of the gates, darting towards me.

"Theo!" I shouted, holding out my arms for an embrace. Little did I know, Theo was not walking towards me for a hug.

"Storm, I'm going to kill you!" he said, flailing his clenched fist against my stomach. A gust of air violently shot from my lungs. Before I could fall onto the rough pavement, Theo held me in his embrace.

"Ouch, that hurt." I squealed. Theo's parents, whom I refrained from speaking to, grinned from the choke of the gates. They carried his belongings in decorative luggage. The family was always dressed with exorbitant fashion, yet they seemed unprepared for this event. Theo's father had noticeable stains on his suit, and his mother's black hair frizzed.

"You didn't tell me that you were here!" Theo criticized.

"Forget that, Theo. The health checkups are the reason why we are here. You messed this all up."

Theo pushed me from his hug and moved to Jem. His hair was poorly brushed, and his black sleepwear looked unwashed.

"You have lots of explaining to do!" he taunted, pointing his finger at Jem. His hand was a foot from her face, and I was almost certain it would strike her unconscious. Jem's masked guard rushed towards Theo, pushing him onto the solid pavement. She remained emotionlessly planted on the ground. I didn't even think she flinched.

"Theo!" denounced his mother. He pretended it was nothing, standing and brushing the coat of sand from his loose sweatshirt.

"Apologize to her, now!" Her scolding tone was so high pitched, I wanted to cover my ears. I stepped back from the hardening conflict. There were already too many to bear. After several arid seconds, Theo locked eyes with Jem.

"I'm sorry," he groaned like a child's forced apology. Jem continued to stand in her frozen pose, finally taming Theo's anger.

"You should be thanking me, not raising your voice at me," she said.

"Please, tell us what this mandatory recruitment is for." his soft-toned father asked, abruptly changing the subject. I wished Grandpa would do something like that for me. Instead, Grandpa would have scolded me for hours on end.

Jem stepped into the center of the circle and projected her voice to the small party.

"To keep it short and sweet, we have recruited six thousand of the healthiest humans to this mission." She pointed to the three towering spaceships. "Theo, Storm, you two are of the lucky six thousand pioneers that will be taking the first manned flight to the Alpha Centauri solar system to the nearest habitable planet, Tau."

"Bu-but, that is over four light years away,"
Theo's father said. He used to be an astronomer, and
his fact was left undisputed. Jem nodded her head,
sympathetically smiling. Personally, I did not believe
Jem was capable of sympathy. After obliterating half
of Niamey with poisonous weaponry, she proved her
power for a malignant purpose.

"Right…our spaceships are fueled from
nuclear propulsion, which means the journey will take
approximately one hundred years to complete," she
said. "These two brave men, alongside the thousands
of their colleagues will be asleep and preserved
throughout the journey."

Theo's mother dropped her son's luggage.
Tears rolled down her cheeks. She rushed to Theo's
loose, shocked state, holding him tightly.

"I will not see my Theo again?" she sobbed. I
watched Grandpa, who remained emotionless. Jem
paced over to Theo's mother, placing a hand on her
shoulder.

"These men are taking part in a crucial
moment for humanity. Earth has no future for them.
It is no longer going to be habitable. Please, go
somewhere rural if you want to survive what is to
come."

I felt the blood rush to my cheeks. Grandpa
always told me to take care of him on his one

hundredth birthday, but I could no longer do that. I opened my arms and rushed to Grandpa, hugging him.

"I'm sorry, Grandpa," I said.

"Sorry for what?" he smiled. "You are a part of something big, Storm!"

"Grandpa, you don't need to talk to me like that. I am older than that." I coughed, too exhausted to cry. He slapped my shoulder, forcing out a laugh. Police cyborgs snatched Theo's dropped luggage.

"Say your farewells now. I need you to report to your designated cabins. You two are the last to come to the party," Jem said, walking to the spaceships. I was worried about Grandpa's safety. I wanted him to be happy, surrounded by those he loved for the remained of his years.

"Grandpa, what will you do?" I asked.

"I know this one place where my old friends live." He glanced around for eavesdroppers and began whisper. "It's an underground shelter for the elderly in Alaska. I will enjoy the remainder of my days there." He elbowed my hanging shoulder. "I'm very proud that you are doing this."

Theo's suited father stood beside me and spoke for the first time in years.

"Be nice to Theo on the trip, son," he said. I jerked my head towards him, pinning a grin on my face.

"He means the world to me," I said, watching Theo, numbed and stuck in his mother's embrace.

"I hope you find somewhere safe to go," I added.

"We know some places." He seemed gloomy and lost. As Jem stated, most people would perish in what was to come. I didn't want to witness the atrocities. The last thing I wanted Grandpa to see was my sentimental vulnerability.

"Hurry up!" Jem shouted from the distance. I latched onto Grandpa for a final time. He laughed, dropping his walking stick to the ground. From my childhood to twenty-two years of age, he was hard to let go. Denial ensued me believe that I would visit him again, soon.

"Grandpa, I won't disappoint you, I promise." My voice trembled. I struggled to hold onto my composure like the crumbling nation itself.

"Make me and your mother proud, Storm," he said. "I wrote this letter to you."

I let go of him as he handed me a brown envelope. I grabbed it, struggling to say the final word, my final farewell.

"Goodbye, Grandpa," I pecked his cheek. He continued to smile. Grandpa was proud of me, and that was all that mattered. I clenched to the sealed envelope, turned around, and walked to the spaceships. My vision hazed in the tears that seeped from my eyes. I briefly glanced over my shoulder for a final time to see Grandpa sob.

CHAPTER THIRTEEN

My leather boots thumped on the concrete floor, each step bringing me closer to the reality of my sealed fate. My lungs were short of breath, looped in amounting stress.

Loud steps trailed behind me. Theo followed my lead. His head hung low like a droplet that struggled to clench onto a leaf. I continued to hold tightly to Grandpa's envelope. The engraining image of Grandpa's smile remained sharper than the view of the floor itself.

"Storm." Theo motioned me to halt. I curtailed my pace, letting him catch up with me. I scanned his expression of desperation and shock. I wrapped my arm around him, rubbing his low hanging arm.

"Theo, I am always here," I comforted. "I am with you."

"I wouldn't know what I'd do without you," he responded.

"I wouldn't know either," I said under my breath. We didn't bother to look back again as we continued walking towards the spaceships. The clutter of space shuttles on their small landing pads came to an end, revealing the bases of the towering yellow, magenta, and black spaceships. The bases of the spaceships widened like a fixated pyramid.

They were as wide as a stadium from the base and taller than most structures I had witnessed in the Chicago skyline. It was a spectacular engineering project, more advanced than anything I had seen before. Three lanky staircases led to a color-coded spaceship. Their engines began to puff out smoke. The rattling from them became louder with every passing second.

I surveyed the metal, reflective staircases, and I squinted in the intensity of the sun's reflection on them. Jem waved her hand in the entrance of the black spaceship. The open-air staircase to her level seemed to be over ten stories tall. My hand continued to latch onto Theo's.

"I don't want to go," he said.

"We don't have any other choice, Theo," I replied. I tried to hold onto every subtle thought that Grandpa would be safe somewhere. I had no one else to care for other than Theo. Meanwhile, Theo had hundreds of relatives he was leaving behind in pending worldwide obliteration.

"I didn't even get to say goodbye," he said, pulling against my grasp.

"Stop!" I scolded; my voice cracked. I let go of Theo's shoulder and pointed at the two masked cyborg officers, trailing us. "You are going nowhere, and I am going nowhere too. The only place we belong is on that ship."

Theo looked around and swung low again in what looked like defeat. He wasn't the only felt that way. I scurried to the top of the staircase, watching Jem's frantic hand motions. Creaks came from the metal staircases. Theo struggled to follow suit, leaning on the metal railing. The engines' roars were too amplified for my sensitive ears, causing me to hold them. Soreness was layered on top of my weak legs from the flight of stairs at the Tenbrook Tower. It happened to be a nightmare reliving itself.

"Jump inside!" Jem shouted. I began to sprint past her, jumping inside the darkened interior of the spaceship. Suddenly, my body gravitated towards the wall.

I looked around to see a row of militarized cyborg security personnel lined the walls. I stood up, still baffled by my feet's placement on the wall. I looked behind to see Jem and Theo lifting themselves off the ground. Behind them, the black door was sideways. Security personnel behind Theo shut the door of access, leaving us as the final passengers to board the black spaceship.

"Manmade gravity is fun to play with," Jem said, observing my dumbfounded face. "Now, follow me!"

I looked at the sealed sideway door for several seconds. I missed my chance. I missed my chance to savor the smell of Earth and feel the sun press my skin. It was all taken for granted until this very last moment. Theo and Jem weren't stopping for me; I had to catch up to them. The three of us paced the darkened hallway with lifeless security cyborgs standing shoulder to shoulder. Wires connected to the over one hundred security guards as they charged.

"You are so tense around them. What are you hiding?" Jem watched Theo.

"I'm not tensed from that," he replied. "I just want to go home, that's all."

"Well, this is your home. The sooner you get used to it, the better," she said. Her purple uniform was stained and roughed up. She looked more tired than when we first met her. I was too curious to learn about what happened.

"Is everything okay, Jem?" I questioned. Jem darted her restless, cold eyes to mine.

"Ha," she said, "you need to be careful about what you ask."

"I'm sorry," I replied, distancing myself from her. She must have gotten into a physical brawl or woke up on the wrong side of her bed. Whatever it was, it would be left in the docket of questions that would remain unanswered.

We approached a thin metal door. I observed all sources of light, dangling from the ceiling. Their illumination was sucked up by the black walls, but the sounds of chatting echoed. Jem pushed open the loose, unlocked door. Hundreds of passengers sat in their seats, and the windows displayed the sun's filtered warmth. Passengers seemed comfortable in their spacious seating. Pangaean people of all kinds and walks of life were recruited, but not in the last minute like Theo and me. Most passengers seemed like they were in their twenties or thirties. Many were athletic and in shape. This was natural selection not decided by nature.

"Sit anywhere," Jem said before weaving between seats. She smiled at some of the passengers as she rushed her way to the front. Theo and I glanced at each other and continued walking for empty seats.

"Over there," he said. I stepped through the row of several emotionally befuddled individuals. Some were sobbing while others were babbling and chuckling. Believing in Jem's words, I was subtly grateful. An opportunity to be human pioneers on another solar system was one to anticipate for. Who knew what we would find? Would we find new species? Aliens?

Despite the anguish of losing Grandpa, I was carrying out my mother's message by partaking in this mission, I sat down on the plush, black seating. The clattering continued, yet Theo and I sat without a peep. I had nothing more to say to him. Pride kept me together. After several minutes of observing the skyline of New York City, the sandy landscape, and the grey, smoggy skies, I locked my gaze at a pink hovermobile lifting and departing from the parking lot. A smile cracked on my face. Now my hovermobile belonged to Grandpa.

"How are you happy?" Theo said, observing me from the corner of his eye. I brought my eyebrows together and opened my mouth. Before I could convey a response to Theo, speakers from the ceiling hushed everyone on board.

"Good Morning!" Jem's recognizable voice rang from the speakers. *"I am Jem Hata. I am going to be your captain on this spaceship."*

Theo and I looked at each other, eye to eye. With her as a captain, there was not much positivity to anticipate.

"Please remain silent and respectful for other guests on this historic flight. At 2 pm, we are scheduled to lift off. Buckle your seats and rest your head on the headrest. The moment we pass the Moon, you will be able to leave this seated section and make way to your designated rooms for preservation. Thank you for partaking in this crucial mission for humanity and

137

Pangaea. "From the position of the sun, I could tell it was eleven in the morning. For three hours, I had to seal my lips and survey the beautiful world to be left behind. All that I felt was the warmth of the seating with the spikes of apprehension.

CHAPTER
FOURTEEN

Time began to slow down. Jem warned passengers several times as the countdown to liftoff ended.

"Good afternoon, passengers. It seems like we have reached our scheduled liftoff. In thirty seconds, we will takeoff. Again, be cautious to equip your buckle. Thank you!"

I gazed at Theo, suspended. He was lifelessly gazing at the row of seats ahead of him. He buckled his seat without a word.

"I'm sorry you have to go through this," I said. Theo looked at me and forced a grin on his sorrowful face. Masked security cyborgs emerged from their charging stations in the back, attempting to smell any hint of lawlessness.

"The ten second countdown begins, now!" Jem announced.

Beep...beep...beep... I threw on my loose buckle and pressed my head on the headrest, hardly excited to leave orbit. The cyborg personnel planted their feet on the ground, maybe magnetizing their themselves to it.

Beep...beep...beep... Theo choked his eyes while I kept mine open. As I looked outside from the corner of my eye, my heart began to race.

Beep...beep...beep...beep. I go numb, feeling a force push me back, pressing me against the plush seating with a pressure that made my head ache. I couldn't twitch a muscle. Everything glued to the seat.

All the seats rattled, shaking me like a maraca. The corner of my eyes caught shockwaves from the lift. It sent stationary space shuttles of all sizes from their launch pads to the sand, breaking into fragments. This launch destroyed the largest space station in the world. I felt Theo's hand clutch my shoulder. His tangerine hair shook over his head like a mop shaking off its liquid residue.

"When will it stop?" I shrieked, deafened from the commotion. Theo remained silent with his eyes shut. If I failed to hear myself, there was no possibility that Theo could have heard my squeals. I closed my eyes as the rattling faded after a hellish minute. Despite overcoming the uncertainty of an unstable acceleration, I was immobilized for what I would witness outside the window. Curiosity counterbalancing fear, I turned my head and watched the astonishing scenery.

"Theo!" I cried, "Look at this!" Hundreds of passengers unbuckled their seatbelts and launched themselves towards the windows. A light blue ocean fused with a grey landscape was all that remained to view on the horizon. It would be the last time that I saw it.

"It's so pretty," A passenger said, leaning too close to us. Security cyborgs stomped their feet on the ground and held their pistols in hand, ordering discipline. In a flash, passengers darted back into their seats. I wondered why they decided to choose mild weaponry, but then, the ship was only thick enough to endure a heavy weapon. Jem commented on the spectacle.

"Passengers, we have officially left Earth's orbit, and we will be passing the moon momentarily. If you believe in a higher power, pray to her for protection on this historic journey."

Theo puffed a gust of wind, exasperated. I ignored Jem's unfavorable request as my eyes observed the stars of the darkened atmosphere. Earth seeped away from the window's display, and the stars resonated brighter by the second. From the ground, it was nearly impossible to catch a glimpse of them. This was what ancient tales spoke of. Stars were once crucial for the survival and movement of humanity. Whenever I looked up at the sky from the ground, not even one would be found; the smog would blanket it.

I jumped in my seat as magenta ship advanced beside us. Hundreds of passengers were gazing outside their tinted windows, and so was I. It was propelled by a dim exhaust.

"Pioneers on board mission Alpha Centauri, your captain Jem Hata, speaking again. This spaceship is approaching the moon and its glass domed cities. After we pass

this vulnerable space, you may have the clearance to access your rooms and preserve your beautiful selves for this hundred-year journey."

While the moon came to visibility, I saw the domes reflect the sun. I locked my focus on the tiny bubbles. Their transparency revealed the buildings and greenery on the other side. Every bubble held a miniature city. The wealthy would dwell in these areas, spending a lifetime viewing the stars.

"Oh shit," Theo said, leaning into the oval window. I looked around the domes for answers, finding it in the heavy cracks of the thick, glassed domes. Blocks of fragmented glass orbited around the moon, and a few lights behind the domes remained flickering. My stomach turned at the sight of it.

"It is most unfortunate that the brutality of Neo-Revolutionaries makes its way two hundred and thirty thousand miles away," Jem added. Passengers gazed out their windows, some covering their mouths.

"Who knows how many families had to suffocate in those domes because of this stupid war?" Theo added, whispering.

"Look," I placed my hand over his, "none of it matters anymore."

"We have left the Moon's orbit. Please make a single file line towards the exits and scan your finger into the identifier machine. You will receive your key to your room to take your needed slumber."

142

Others moved to make a line to their rooms, but I dug into my pocket for the letter Grandpa handed to me. I felt nothing but the residue of fabric. I patted down legs for a clue, scurrying my eyes around the floor. I opened the seal of my lips.

"Oh yeah," Theo said. "While you were running up the stairs to get inside this spaceship, you dropped an envelope."

"Did you get it?" I locked eyes with Theo. He seemed like he understood the importance of it.

"The wind took it, and I wasn't even thinking about it. I'm so sorry," he said. I leaned back into the plush seating, holding my hand to the temples of my head. My frail heart thumped. I would never know what Grandpa wrote to me.

CHAPTER
FIFTEEN

"Do you want to go now?" Theo asked, tugging my shoulder. I was not keeping track of time or anything for that matter.

"No," I mumbled, looking out the window. Each second of pondering dug me deeper into a hellish regret. Maybe Grandpa just wrote a short farewell; maybe he spewed out every piece of information to stuff my clueless void.

"No one is here, Storm," he said, placing his hand on my shoulder. "Let's get out of here."

I turned away from the window, observing the eerie bodies of seating. Security cyborgs remained planted on the ground, scanning the large cabin. My eyes met the masked cyborg, and it scooped its hand, ushering us to scurry.

"Okay," I said, launching myself up too fast. My head and perception began to turn, and I slumped back into the seat, making Theo giggle. Maybe if I clowned around more, he would lighten up. Momentarily, I could forget about what was lost at home. I made a second attempt to pull myself up, my overused quadriceps trembled to straighten. Theo's grey eyes met mine.

"Are you sure you can walk?" he laughed. I smiled and brushed past him. We navigated through the linear row of seating and into the walkway up to the vast spaceship. My leather boots rubbed against the black carpeting, brushing off residue sand: what was left of Earth. A hefty exit door stood ahead of us. Theo slowed his pace, but I threw myself onto the door. I let out a gust of air and bounced back.

"You're definitely not okay." Theo laughed again, turning to a soda dispenser sized identifier machine beside the door. He pressed his finger on the vast touch screen, and his full name appeared on the screen in a bold font. The rest of the screen was eventually pixilated to display a swiveling, natural, third dimensional version of Theo in white clothes.

"Wow," I mumbled at the display.

"What?" Theo questioned, darting his eyes down at me. Theo's synthetic dyes were unveiled on the screen, displaying the true DNA replication of him. The figure in the display had brown hair, brown eyes, and a cheeky smile. The Theo standing beside me had fabricated, grey eyes, tangerine hair, and skin cloaked in insecurity.

"I just think you look better over there." I pointed my finger at the digital display. He struggled to view the screen like the sun to the eyes. Since his childhood, Theo twisted and turned to the acceptance of society, but not to himself.

"That's funny," he said, stepping towards the small shoot beside the screen, barbing a keycard.

"No," I said, halting him in his tracks. "You are a beautiful person. I never doubted that."

Theo smiled with a resonating glow, something genuine I haven't seen in years. He stepped aside to observe himself in his natural form.

"You know what?" Theo increased his pitch in tone. "I look pretty darn good like that, huh?"

He snapped awake from his fabricated self-love and snatched the keycard from the shoot. The keycard waved in front of the barricaded door. In the blink of an eye, the door drew up. Like a hotel, hundreds of rooms neighbored each other on the other side of the hefty door.

"Where is your room?" I asked.

"Um..." he lifted the keycard to eye level. "Level three, room seven."

"Will you wait for me to get my card?"

"It's a hundred years, but it will feel like one night." He slapped my chest. "I will basically see you tomorrow."

Before he darted to his designated room, I stopped him again.

"Um," I hesitated. Theo turned around to hear me. "Just be safe for me, will you?"

"Of course, I will. See you later." He sped away from the closing door like he recognized the mapping of the trail ahead. Gone, just like that. He didn't think twice about it.

For one hundred years, Theo and I would no longer see each other. But who was I kidding? We were no longer on Earth, and Earth would soon face destruction. Time is manmade which meant that the passengers on board these spaceships were the only ones to grasp the concept of time. Since all of us would be asleep in the meanwhile, no one would endure time's passage. Therefore, Theo was right: being preserved for a century would make this lengthy journey feel like an overnight slumber.

I impatiently pressed my finger on the bulky machinery, letting the hefty screen sample my DNA. I was curious to see myself in a third dimensional character. My toes inched away from the screen and I chewed on my lip. Suddenly, my character appeared on the screen. A figure with brown eyes, black hair combed to the side spun around the screen. Hairs on the back of my neck rose, understanding Theo's distaste in looking at himself.

Click! A card popped out of the machine, and I plucked it with my still numb hands. I scanned the numbers on the card.

Floor one, room fifty. I was hoping that I would be on the same floor as Theo. We could have been neighbors for a century. I smirked at the silliness of the idea and waved my card towards the door. The door opened to an empty hallway, making me wonder how long Theo and I remained in our seats.

I looked at the cyborg officers in the distance behind me. They were observing me as if I were the last wake passenger. Maybe I was, and that sent another chill down my spine. I scurried away from the door and kept my senses aware for room number fifty. Vintage styled doors revealed their numbers in an almost unrecognizable calligraphy.

one

five

twenty

forty

I slowed my pace, and like a mosquito to light, I was attracted towards the gleaming wooden door: room number fifty. I waved the key in the face of the door and it clicked open.

I grinded my teeth together and my fingertips felt the cool metal doorknob. I grasped the handle, swiveled it, and pulled towards me. Dark walls blended into the hallway. A single dim-lit light resonated from the ceiling. Some walking closets were bigger than this. The room hardly had breathing space. In the corner lied a coffin-like preservation bed and my valueless bags of belongings. Digital numbers hung on the wall.

Minute: 47

Hour: 2

Day: 1
Week: 1
Month: 1
Year: 1

It must have been a count of the journey's length. At one hundred years, this digital clock on the wall may be my alarm clock to gain consciousness. A vintage music player of mine was hanging from the side of my bag. I lowered myself and snatched the player. It featured natural melodies of nature and birds. Whenever I needed help sleeping, I always tuned in. A pair of headphones were wrapped around the player, ready to use. A speaker embedded in the ceiling turned on.

"Passengers, this is your captain, Jem, once again. If you have not been preserved yet, this is your first and final warning to do so in ten minutes. After ten minutes, all sources of light will be eliminated to save some energy. If you find yourself awakening mid-journey because of any glitch, please set yourself back to preservation. Thank you, and enjoy."

A commanding rumble in my stomach and fatigue persuaded me to hibernate the pain away. I lifted the coffin-like preservation bed's cover and observed its material. It was thin, almost seeming uncomfortable. Fortunately for me, sleep was a luxury that I desired. I kicked off my leather boots and threw myself into the bed, feeling the tension in my legs release. My hand pulled the handle above me, tightening the already condensed air.

Compressed and mildly claustrophobic, this was the environment I would have to spend a century in. My hands unraveled and untangled the headphones, and I utilized the screen of the music player as a source of light, viewing the components of the preservation bed's hood. The only components I saw was a foolishly big green and red button. A rational guess was that pressing red would be an emergency stop, and the green initiated my preservation. I plugged in my earbuds and hit play. Sounds that were once taken for granted began to melodize in my eardrums.

I punched the green button. Birds chirped as the ocean brushed on the beach in the background. Thick gases seeped from above. I chewed on the gas, unable to taste its numbing flavor. Although I was never placed in such a situation, I embraced the cool gas into my lungs.

I let it carry me to sleep.

CHAPTER SIXTEEN

I opened my eyes, certain it was only a blink. That was only until my hand brushed off a residue of thin slime from the palm of my hand. It must have been landing time, and I had to rush to witness this moment. It took strength to push open the rusty lid over me. I turned my stiff eyes to the digital clock on the wall.

> Minute: 35
> Hour: 7
> Day: 4
> Week: 3
> Month: 8
> Year: 40

It must have been a simple glitch, but I needed to have some time to recollect. The thought of Grandpa arose. He must have passed away by now, hopefully by something natural. It was no longer an issue of the matter. Grandpa was gone, but he would always be alive and well in my head.

Who knew what Earth looked like? Maybe the world was a ruin. Pondering didn't give me any solid answers.

My back descended onto the bedding, and I shut the lid. I punched the green button and unhooked the dead music player from my slimy ears. After several lengthy seconds in the frigid capsule, the lack of gasses was questionable.

I threw open the lid again, kicked my feet onto the ground, and attempted to stand. Faint sounds of clattering bounced from the hallways. The pitch-black room was nearly impossible to navigate. Tangled black bags came under the soles of my feet. I held out my hand, attempting to meet the door's handle. Scuffles became louder like someone running with brick shoes.

"Passengers, sorry to awaken you." Jem's voice was restless and stunned. *"This spaceship is under a mild lockdown. You must lock your doors as soon as possible."* Obviously, Jem must have woken the entire spaceship for this. I was aghast that this would be the first conflict that this journey faced. There were asteroids, mechanical issues; heck, even aliens could come and wipe us clean.

I felt the handle of the door, attempting to sense any lock in the pitch-dark room. A dusty, wooden door with a cold handle were the only objects in my contact. Picturing myself entering the room, I only observed the exterior of the room when the lights were on. I didn't quite remember a lock.
Despite it, the sounds of footsteps grew through the hallways, and my heart began to race.

Thump... Thump... Thump! The potential threat grew louder with every second, ushering me to panic. Heavy feet lined up outside the door. There was no place to hide. A hand landed on the door handle, twisting the unlocked knob. I held my breath and leaped towards the door hinges. With the door squeaking open, I pressed my back on the wall behind me. Boots thumped on the rough flooring, entering the miniscule and pitch-black room. Palpitations in my chest were louder than the thoughts running through my head. I held my hand over my mouth, breathing slowly through my nose. The room was too silent though the invisible figure stepped on a plastic bag. He cussed under his breath and kicked the bag towards me. I winced as the bag hit my chest.

Finally, the figure lifted my preservation's cover and cussed again. I mistakenly elbowed the wall behind me. My breath froze; my eyes stopped moving. His deep footsteps turned around and trailed towards me.

I needed to flee; I needed to fight. While I thought of what turn to take, the lights flickered back on, flaring my sensitive eyes. After the brief adjustment, I looked in the shadow of a man that stood a foot from my face. Although he had no mask, all I faced was a silhouette. He was as big as the man who chased Theo and me in the empty streets of Chicago.

A puff of his breath almost brushed my hair. He held no weapon, besides his fists. Speechless, petrified, and anxious, I whispered.

"Who are you?"

The man jolted towards the door, hauled open its frail handle, and sprinted into the empty hallway. Like a statue, I stood tensely frozen beside the door. I scanned the passageway to see a lock on top of the door. My arms latched onto the lock and swiveled it to a click. Clothes scattered on the floor. After a minute of contemplating the situation that passed, the speakers above delivered a message.

"After you lock your doors, you have my clearance to begin sleeping again."

I locked my eyes on a piece of paper tucked under my grey sweater. It wasn't there before. I plucked the paper from the floor, feeling the tension of stretching on my fragile back. Black, handwritten letters were plastered all over it.

Dear Storm,

We, the Revolutionaries need your help! Jem Hata is not to be trusted, and the values of Pangaea must come to an end. We need you to represent us, as you mother represented peace twenty years ago. Avenge your mother and join our movement to build a new world of freedom, liberty, and democracy. If you want to take this offer of change, Storm Raleston, crumple this letter and leave it outside your door after the lights go out.

Sincerely, the Neo-Revolutionaries.

I threw the paper on the floor, but after several minutes of pacing the room, I contemplated the benefits and detriments. Maybe the Neo-Revolutionaries on board this ship knew something I didn't know. Maybe answers would finally come to my fingertips.

But what if this was just a trap? If I were caught, I would be executed on the spot without a sliver of mercy.

Once more, I plucked the letter from the floor. My eyes scanned the letter several times, and as any rash decision I made the past several days, I crumpled it.

CHAPTER SEVENTEEN

*K*nock! *Knock!*

"This is Pangaean security. Please open your preservation room."

I tucked the letter into my pocket, forming a noticeable lump. I scurried towards the door and opened it to two deep-voiced security cyborgs. They were identically buff and masked in black.

"What's up?" I asked, blocking the view to the scattered display of intrusion.

"Are you safe?" one of the guards asked, leaning in. I couldn't tell which one was talking to me.

"Yes, I was going to go preserve myself, but you two arrived." I slouched by the door and conceded to a swelling nonchalant environment.

"I see that you're sweating," one of them noted. "Why may this be?"

I began to observe the trails of sweat streaming from my forehead. Nervousness drew the sides of my lips up, fabricating my best attempt at a smile.

"Well," I rushed, "this room is a little humid." I froze, repenting my blunder of words.

"We need to conduct a scan in this room then," said one of the bulky cyborgs. This meant everything, including me, would be checked. I needed to hide the letter elsewhere before it was too late. While one of the security cyborgs struggled to push forward, I remained frozen behind the door.

"Mr. Raleston, comply or face punishment!" They drew their pistols from their pockets. My heart skipped a beat and I stepped aside. The squeaking door revealed an array of scattered trauma. They immediately began to brush the clothes away from their feet like they were searching for a particular thing.

My hands lowered and blanketed the lump from my pocket. I pressed my back on the wall beside the preservation bed. This room was too small one being, let alone three. Most terrifying of all, I didn't know what the cyborg security was communicating with each other. Radio signals kept the conversation far from a suspect's ears. Both cyborgs turned their back to me but locked eyes with mutuality.

"Mr. Raleston, have you seen a sheet of paper anywhere?" one of them demanded; they kept their backs towards me.

"No," I replied. A rashness pushed me to dig into my pocket and whip out the crumpled ball of paper. It was in my hand, and I attempted to lower it to the ground without either of them noticing. I squatted and looked down, placing the paper on the ground. I looked back up to see two pistols pointing in my direction.

I failed at attempting to think of an excuse; my heart raced to articulate. One cyborg leaped towards me, snatching the paper from the ground. It unraveled the letter and scanned its contents. I opened my mouth, attempting to explain.

"Mr. Raleston," they said together, "you are under arrest for possessing Neo-Revolutionary material." It crumpled the paper again. I rose my hands and expressionlessly spoke for a final time.

"This is not what it looks like! It was on the ground! I was picking it up!"

"Say one more word and I will kick your pathetic face!" replied the security cyborg. I sealed my mouth, trembling. The man who was in my room earlier must have been a cyborg himself, cracking down on an individual like me.

I faced the black wall and embraced it. My hands were clenched with agonizing force. Frigid, metal handcuffs suffocated my wrists. I was tugged in several directions into the eerie hallway.

"I know how to walk," I whimpered. Suddenly, a force threw me towards the wall. I gritted my teeth as the pain in my shoulder pushed me on the carpeted floor.

"I told you to shut up!" the masked cyborg shouted.

"Please," I said, aspiring to stand. Doors on the floor clicked open. Observing eyes cowardly aimed towards the abuse of security. "Please don't kill me," I added, raising my hands towards the ceiling. Maybe my life would be saved if everyone was watching. Cyborgs know how to think twice.

"Kill the Neo-Revolutionist!" someone shouted, hidden behind the crack of the door. My chest collapsed at the sound of it.

"Don't kill him, you scum!" one added.

"Long live the revolution!" said another.

Divisions grew amongst bickering passengers, filling the dim-lit hallway with the white noise. The cyborgs attempted to cultivate the source of revolutionary chants. I limped towards the nose of the spaceship. The last door in the hallway was the size of a spec, maybe a half-mile or more away. I was heading there anyways. I may as well have made my pleas to Jem.

The corner of my senses felt a tremor. Clamor silenced and doors shut closed. I stood baffled, holding my throbbing shoulder. I turned back to see an army of security reinforcement march through the halls. I began to pace faster. My whole body had sharp pains, so running simply wasn't an option.

"Hurry up, Mr. Raleston!" the impatient cyborg said. I kept looking back to see the cyborgs get closer. I scanned the door numbers on the way there.

seventy

one hundred

two hundred fifty

four hundred twenty

The hallway came to an end. A door blocked the way forward; my assumption was that it was the cabin.

Sweat continued to trickle down my face, and a bruise on my shoulder became distinct. Now, I understood the cause of Neo-Revolutionaries. An object had the judgment to harm and kill. Nothing was more distorted than harming an innocent human over the crime of curiosity.

Cyborgs approached the identifier machine ahead of me, one of them waving their keycard in the face of the door. I looked back to see the intimidating army of security slowing their pace and returning to their place of origin. Screeches of friction on rusty metal resonated throughout the tight halls. Their parade of strength was over.

As the door ascended, my eyes met two colossal windows. A warm breeze brushed my skin. I stepped into the spacious room, and I was greeted with hundreds of quotes on the walls in several languages; it sparked Deja-vu.

"Come in." Jem's purple Afro stuck out from the swiveling chair. Her hands sped to tinker with the wide array of controls. "Storm, I am extremely disappointed."

"Jem, you know I am loyal to this nation's future." I crept up to her. She flipped a switch and turned around to observe me. Her eyes squinted with doubtless question. She wore the same purple uniform.

"Then please explain why you had Neo-Revolutionary propaganda in your room?" She barbed her finger towards the two cyborgs behind me. One held out the crumpled ball of paper as a trophy of betrayal.

"You don't understand," I hesitated.

"I think I understand," she said. "Storm, I need your cooperation, especially your honesty."

"What is the big deal with crumpling a wad of paper?" I said.

"Take a seat," she said, motioning to the seat beside her. This spaceship must have been built to be operated by two people. I touched the cold, dusty swiveling chair. It was evident that this second captain didn't exist. A countless number of stars lit the windows like vibrant glitter.

"I could stay awake for a century, and that display would never get old." Jem surveyed the image for several seconds. She then turned back towards me.

Her lips clamped together, covering her misaligned teeth. "I have been awake for several hours, and I was awakened to know that some passengers were awake to make these handwritten letters. Storm, this ship doesn't have enough power to shine a light for years, let alone have a functional security camera. Solar panels receiving starlight are only used for the core functions of this ship and emergencies like the one we are in." She wove to the lights above me. Their circular shape illuminated warmth in darkness.

"So, you guys didn't write these letters to set people up?" I asked.

"No, and we are trying to figure out who these people are. If their recruitment grows over the next several decades, this ship will be under serious threat."

"That doesn't sound good at all," I added, hoping that she believed I was on her side.

"Anyways, you must have crumpled that paper to get some answers on your mother."

"What?" I shook awake from the widow's captivating display.

"Storm, I understand you are frustrated for the truth." She waved her hand in the security, escorting them from the room. "In a matter of fact, I knew your mother."

"I don't know if I can trust anything you tell me anymore." I pulled my shoulders back, silencing myself.

"For this one time, Storm, please trust what I tell you," she pleaded, an emotional appeal rare to my eyes. I perceived Jem as a heartless woman, but she seemed to have dug extensively to find her hidden emotions. "Your mother and I were great friends."

I shook my head. As much as I yearned to shut her up, I kept silent to hear the fairy tale.

"Please continue." I slouched on the cool backrest.

"I believe you were only a baby when she was working on a controversial peace deal between early Neo-Revolutionaries and the government. Every warning that she received from the cyber council to end peace negotiations pushed her to try harder. She was so close to sealing a peace agreement, but that was only until she was arrested for treason."

I already heard this portion of the story from Grandpa, which was a well-known truth. He would never fabricate such a story. My lifeless eyes disclosed that reality.

"So, how did you stand for her?" I questioned.

"Well, at first," she clamped her hands together. "I told her that she needed to end the peace negotiations. Unfortunately, your mother was too stubborn to do that."

Jem laughed, and her eyes moistened from the emergence of the memory. I observed her carefully, indecisive on whether her emotions were genuine.

"Whenever the government agencies held international meetings, we always found ourselves bumping into each other and complementing our outfits. We would discuss important legislations that the president favored. The further she pushed, the further I distanced myself from her." She smiled and concluded with a fact that slipped from Grandpa's lips. "Before your mother became a controversial figure, she created this very protocol that we are embarking on. In the case of extreme conflict, this mission would be launched, and humanity would lead an intergalactic expansion of Pangaea. She chose six people, including herself to be the captains of these three ships."

"I am sitting in her seat," I replied, sending a chill in my bones.

"In the case of extreme conflict, your mother and I were supposed to lead together on this journey." She darted her eyes to her purple boots. My lips broke their patient seal.

"Jem, did it ever occur to you that you held meetings with a programmed computer. A programmed digital council decided my own mother's death, and a programmed security cyborg flung me on a wall like a mosquito several minutes ago?"

"You don-"

"No, I completely understand," I said. "Humanity is simply too primitive to decide its own fate."

I tied my legs and placed the palm of my hand on my kneecap. She attempted to articulate, but she seemed to have failed to grasp the content of truth. Corners of her lips pulled down, revealing her disappointment.

"Look at what happened to Earth because of those Neo-Revolutionists." Jem leaned towards me, almost pushing past a comfortable vicinity of space. "In a new world, pioneers such as you and your friend will paint of new picture of human prosperity."

"You sound just like a propaganda mouthpiece."

"Watch it, Storm. In a government protocol, I should have executed you."

I sealed my lips, freezing my breath. As much as my unruly mouth burbled, I was a dead man walking. Jem was the judge, jury, and executioner.

"You look confused." She interrupted my train of thought.

"I am never going to get real answers." I rolled my eyes, preserving a ruthless character. "That's all I ever wanted."

She stood from her seat, creating creases of wisdom on her exposed, dark knees. She leaned on the control panel. I remained apprehensive.

"Remember those pills I gave you?" she said.

"Yeah, of course, I do."

"Those pills were invented by the Pangaean medical agency."

"What does that have to do with anything?"

"Those pills were invented fifty years ago. Did you fail to notice that it healed your injury overnight?" While she paused for a response, I pondered.

"That drug could have saved countless lives, but the government decided to hold off its release to the public because it would drop tax revenue from hospitals and drug companies."

The puzzle began to piece together. Jem kept on reminding Theo and me to receive health checkups because our poor health was obscured from the pill's healing qualities. Our health score was placed in the government database, and that labeled our names in the database as one of Earth's healthiest. Before word of the mission spread, names were drafted in the last minute by the government's database.

"If it was not released to the public, how did you acquire it?" I asked.

"Neo-Revolutionaries took over the agency and reproduced the drug in their isolated lands. I took the initiative to smuggle the drug, even some Adrenalin Juice."

"Why were you trading with them if you were fighting against them?" I brought my eyebrows to the bridge of my nose.

"Our trade deals kept my military base from being overtaken," she said. "If I missed a payment, they said they would attack in twelve hours."

"Our trade deal? Aren't you a traitor if you are making deals with the Neo-Revolutionists?" I stood from my seat. Jem didn't bother to respond to that question. She was guilty by association, and she wasn't going to bother admitting it.

"After you and your friend left the base, the next weekly payment was due. My base lacked the necessary funds, and I began a twelve-hour timer. I planned to warn Carter of what was to come before the attack struck. I would come directly to New York and lead a bloodless mission to Alpha Centauri. Unfortunately, nothing went as I planned. Seven hours later, I woke up to the premature sounds of the base gates barging open. Wires of my cyborg soldiers and the blood of revolutionaries began to spill on base grounds."

I lowered myself back to the seat, preventing to question her further. It seemed hard for her, or that was what she wanted me to think.

"I ordered Carter to replace me as military leader of my base, and he was so terrified." She puffed out, understanding the crime she committed. "I ran, tumbling several times to get to a nearby aircraft. As I fled, Carter intercepted missiles left and right, protecting my flight."

"Jem," I said, beginning to recall Carter and his robotic like motions. My sentence left hanging, unable to think of anything to say. Carter spoke of his family and the countless years spent on the base. His red regalia remained engrained in thought.

"I just want peace," Jem annunciated like she said it a million times before. She sighed again, looking down and shaking her head. It reminded me of Grandpa. Sacrifices needed to be made for survival; this was one of those cases. "So, do me a favor and help me. I want this mission to go smoothly, and most of all, without conflict."

I nodded my head, but I agreed with her this time.

"You're dismissed," she said. My feet tip-toed to the exit, and Jem continued to play with the array of controls, turning away from me. Before I placed my hand on the door's exit button, a bookshelf beside the door caught my attention. It was made of a light-colored wood and held multiple identical copies of several books.

Science of Matter

Biology

Human Extinction on Earth

Human Extinction on Earth? This book had to be written, published, and placed on the ship before launch. Jem mentioned some nuclear war, but a detailed book on it magnetized me for a stronger dosage of answers.

Multiple copies created a channel throughout the shelf's row. Jem wouldn't know if I happened to take one. I looked at her again; her back was still against me. I trailed beside the row of books and plucked the book from the shelf without a pinch of noise. I slipped it under my shirt from the bottom. For a final time, I looked at Jem; she seemed too occupied to notice. Whatever was in this book, I had to read it. My freed hand pressed the exit button while the other grasped the book, blanketed under my shirt. The door slid up, revealing the lengthy hallway. It revived the scarring memory of being thrown against the hallway wall. I was the slightest bit glad that Theo was on another floor, unfazed by what happened. I stepped a foot into the hallway but froze, feeling incomplete.

"Thank you, Jem," I said quietly, "Thank you for caring for us."

I strolled into the hallway, feeling pressure on my chest. My firsts remained clenched. I inhaled a deep breath and carefully exhaled. I had to stop taking foolish risks, yet my curiosity acts first.

After making way into my already unlocked room, I made sure that the door behind was sealed and locked. I pulled the book from under my shirt. It was roughly two hundred pages, and the front cover displayed a picture of the grey planet that was left behind. My thumb flipped to a random page, displaying an array of words too small to comfortably read.

During World War Two, divided humans killed millions over an ideology. Mankind showed its true colors of violence, savagery, and conquest.

True, but as a history student, I knew that the allies were attempting to repel a tyrant force. This book had an obscurity of words, pressing me towards the question. I flipped to another page, trying to find the correlation between title and text.

The world had over two hundred nations, and it all came to one: Pangaea. Overtime, the digital president became increasingly self-aware with updates. His awareness led him to eliminate his flawed human staff.

My jaw dropped. It all made sense now; mother died because the president believed humans weren't enough to run the government. It found a way to eliminate my mother when she was working for a greater good. If the government continued to function without opposition, Jem would have been dead too.

I flipped towards the end of the book, skimming the final passage in the book. My lips moved to every paragraph, every word. The title of this book was finally linked to a passage in the end. I let go of the pages, letting it land on the pile of clothes on the ground.

The lights began to dim to a close, but I had to rush before it was pitch dark. I tore a blank page from the book and scurried to pull out a pen from my baggage. I pressed the page to a wall and began to write, giving my best impression of it.

This is Storm Raleston. I have crucial information that the people must know.

Before I crumpled the note, plopped it outside the door, and drifted into coma, I added a final line in the pitch dark, hoping that it was comprehensible.

Yes, I am willing to join the Neo-Revolutionaries.

CHAPTER
EIGHTEEN

I gasped for air, pushing in whatever I could into my lungs. A rush of panic began to fling my hand around for the red button. I must have been choking on the gasses. I was unable to shout; my trembling hands continued to search for release.

Wheezing replaced with silence. My ears didn't detect a sound other than my racing heart. My eyes remained clenched. Images of Grandpa, Theo, and Jem appeared in flashes. Maybe it was over; I was a dead piece of meat several trillion miles away from home. No one would have known I was dead until we landed.

Would I be a pile of bones by then?

I hoped so. The thumping of my heart slowed, tranquility replacing panic. People had to know what was in the book, and it would all be lost and gone.

Suddenly, my uncontrollable hands clasped a circle piece of plastic, and the lid over me flung open. I sucked in air from the cool room, piercing my tender chest. Dry and cold, the wind in my lungs pushed out the thick gasses, but it itched my throat. I coughed, having the urge to throw up. Pitch darkness prevented me from measuring the dizziness ensued on me. A whisper circled around me several times until it became comprehensible.

"Storm, are you okay?"

"What?" I asked, still gasping for air. My eyes looked at the digits on the wall. The blurry numbers twisted and turned into my distorted perception for several seconds until it stabilized.

Minute: 22
Hour: 9
Day: 3
Week: 2
Month: 5
Year: 80

"Who are you?" I asked, hoping that it was a simple hallucination.

"Come with me, please," he whispered back, placing his soft hand on mine. I knew from then that it was not an illusion.

"Who are you?" I asked again.

"No time for questions. You need to come follow me."

I crunched from the bed and continued to grasp onto the mysterious person's hand. I held firmly, assuring this person was anchored onto the floor.

"Are you a Neo-Revolutionary?" I raised my voice.

"Please be quiet."

"Tell me, please! I have so much to tell you!"

"Be quiet, now," he replied. I felt metal press on my forehead. Imagining what was present, uncertainty pictured the worst. For all that I knew, I could have been fooled by a harmless metal rod. My hand unconsciously loosened its grip.

"Okay," I trembled, "you win." I continued to grasp onto his dry hand, lifting myself from the preservation bed.

Coughing one last time for filtered oxygen, a tug on my arm yanked out the muck of gas from my throat. My hand wiped the ground several times until it felt the book lying on the floor.

Like a child, my hand was held by a guardian who knew the way forward. The stranger began to move forward without a hitch, disclosing their familiarity with the track. My door was obviously unlocked, but how that happened was a question that needed to be answered.

I chewed on my lip. The undisclosed location of my destination brought me to mounting worry. My other hand held to the flimsy book. I shut my eyes and focused on the silence of the halls.

"If it makes you walk faster," he whispered, releasing the metal object from pointing at my forehead. A cold ring continued to tickle my head. Playing the game of courtesy, I threw one foot after the other with haste.

"Hey," I whispered, "I'm not your enemy, so please tell me what's happening."

"Just be quiet, okay?" he hissed. I wanted to speak, but the words remained stuck in my throat. Plush carpeting turned to a hard floor. His hand became humid as if I held a warm cup of tea.

We were still on level one, but we made several twists and turns around the spaceship. Everyone was fast asleep, including the captain, so there was no point in being quiet. Even the security personnel were nowhere to be heard. Everything was out but us, which was not a reassuring thought.

"We are here," he whispered. Open windows illuminated by the starlight. The man that held my hand was bulky and very familiar.

"You dropped the letter in my room," I whispered.

"Yeah," he said. His face was rugged and pale. His dark stubble extended past the shadow of his chin. I was terrified of him, and now he was leading the path ahead. Windows lined up the spaced room, shining brighter than I would imagine. A group of several people sat on the floor as if some pagan ritual was about to commence.

"Storm Raleston," a middle-aged man said. He extended his hand to shake mine. I pulled away from the wet grasp of one hand to the next. His soft eyes and blonde hair glistened in the starlight. "I am Keb, president of the Neo-Revolutionaries on all three ships. I was democratically elected, and we read your pleas on paper."

The stench of body odor and dirt radiated from the group of mysterious people. I stopped breathing through my nose.

"And I'm Timothy," said the man who led me, no longer whispering. He pocketed the evident pistol in the back of his pocket.

"Do you know your blood, Storm?" asked Keb, looking more handsome by the second.

"I know," I rushed. "My mother worked as an advisor to the president, and she was executed." I looked at the floor, acting sorrowful. "I know exactly why, but before I do, you need to know something even more important." I lifted the book and flipped to the last page.

"Where did you get that from?" Keb asked.

"I swiped it from the captain," I said. "This was one of the non-fiction titles that I had to look at."

I struggled to read every word under the dim stars from the window, but I remembered the words with more clarity.

"Three spaceships of healthy humans left, leaving Earth behind. Neo-Revolutionaries on Earth later prove themselves as victorious, but the good faith of Pangaea was never going to let that happen. Two weeks after the spaceships left Earth, a mechanism began, obliterating every inch of Earth's crust. If Pangaea died, so did humankind." I choked out the final words, but they remained in my throat like an irritating rash.

"Who wrote that book?" Keb asked as if the author was my best friend.

"It doesn't say, but I'm guessing a computer did." Computers never took credit for their work, and the nameless book disclosed that.

The circle of revolutionaries began to whisper to each other, but Keb's whispers had a distinct accent.

"Look," Interrupted, "I don't want to believe what is in this book, but it's the only source of answers to what happened on Earth. Pangaea is responsible for a genocide. We're the only ones left."

"You did a great job to share this information with us." Keb looked at everyone, waiting for their approval. He scratched his blonde hair as if he was losing comfort. "For a long time, we thought you were working with Pangaea."

"Oh, it's from that live interview. I had an earpiece, and I was threatened to be shot if I didn't say what Jem wanted me to say." I paused. "Turns out, she was close to assassinating me anyways."

"You are speaking about the sniper?" Keb raised his chin.

"Yeah, why do you ask?" I asked.

177

"I was the sniper," Keb said. "I was aiming for you, but I missed."

Blood rush up to my head. He wanted to *kill* me. This is what it all came down to.

"Why are you telling me this?" I stepped up to Keb, but he didn't flinch. Timothy held his gun in hand and stepped forward.

"I was the guy who chased you down the street with the others." Timothy sounded regretful.

"And I'm supposed to trust any of you because of this?" I wanted to run, far, but I couldn't. The walls began to close.

"No, Storm," Keb lowered his voice to a tone that was almost unrecognizable. "We thought you were working with them because of that news interview, but it turns out that we were completely wrong. We are human, and we regret our faults. I am incredibly sorry." I observed all the quietly perched people from the light of starlight. Some looked worried and others optimistic. Keb placed a hand on my shoulder. "Computers never apologize, and they want us dead. We have to work together, now more than ever."

"Please, give us a second chance and we will prove that we are a force for good," Timothy said. He walked behind me and wrapped his bulky arm around me like I was his friend.

"Then what do you want from me now?" I said, buckling under the pressure.

"Most of us wake up during scheduled periods every twenty years to discuss our game plan," Keb answered. "This time interval has lasted three days, but we are ending in two."

"So, five days of eating nothing?" I asked casually, pressing a clenched fist to my stomach. Keb observed me; his straight-cut hair stayed fixated on his forehead.

"Timothy, give him a dosage of vitamins."

"Yes, sir," he said, darting somewhere in the pitch dark. After several seconds, he emerged with a cup of water and an almost empty dropper. He stood in front of me and leveled the dropper on top of the water.

Blop! The clear droplet transformed the clear water into a brown color. It looked like some kind of food coloring. Timothy's arm extended towards me, but I remained stiff.

"Um," I hesitated, "what is that?"

"That's the gas you have been breathing in for the last eighty years," Keb replied. "This is a drink worth three thousand calories, and it has all the basic vitamins for a functioning body.

"All in one drop?" I grabbed the glass cup, swirling around the brown mixture. "Is that even possible?"

179

"The Pangaean government kept all scientific advancements in the dark." Keb shook his head. "We poked a hole in the mineral tank and extracted a gallon to survive. Little did we know; a gallon would last us a year."

I tipped the edge of the glass on my lower lip and sipped the brown drink. It tasted like sour rotten meat mingled with spoiled milk. I shut my eyes and moved the glass away from me.

"Chug it or it will taste worse," Timothy said. I gritted my teeth, lifted the drink over my mouth again, and began to pour all of its contents into every corner of my mouth. Gulp after harsh gulp, the sour and filthy taste clung onto my throat. I tried to ignore it, but it was far too strong. I rested my hand on my knees, ready to vomit.

"It's always hard at first," someone in the circle added. I tried to smile, but my face had something between a smirk and frown. Keb placed his hand on my shoulder again, but out of irritation, I tugged it away.

"I'm fine," I whispered, breathing from my mouth.

"When you need to take a piss, do it in the bowl over there," Timothy added.

"Why?"

"Well, we will filter th-"

"Did I just drink someone's urine?"

"Um," he hesitated, "yes, but its filtered"

"Oh shit," I said, feeling the drink move back up, forming a lump in my throat. I kept my mouth shut, attempting to yank the image away from my mind.

Don't puke. Don't puke. Don't puke, was all that I could have thought of. After several excruciating seconds, I sucked in the filtered air and exhaled. Everyone stood, watching me like I was going to say something important. As much as they anticipated a contributing member, I was anything but that. For all that I could have done, I was hardly able to devour a cup of the solution down my throat.

"How do you keep in contact with the neighboring ships?" I switched the focus from my stomach.

"We are using solar-powered radios, but it's hard to transfer much," Keb whispered. "Using solar power on starlight is virtually the same as using solar power on a moonless night."

"What has gone through though?" I asked.

"We can't tell you everything, Storm," he replied. I looked at everyone else, and their odd smirks on their faces displayed the same message.

"Look," I clarified. "I am inconclusive on where I stand in this situation. If it weren't for the captain of this ship, I wouldn't be here."

"Fair enough, but we need her dead if she thinks that a computer president will be the future of humankind." Keb changed his expression in a heartbeat. He was no longer the good-looking, kind person I saw several minutes ago. It made me take a step back, even a little nonplussed. "If we are going to build a new Pangaea, it will be one of human representation."

Timothy clenched the pistol in his hand as I remained speechless. I could only refute enough before I became a government loyalist.

"Well, it looks like it's bedtime for me." I smiled anxiously.

"We will wake you up in twenty years. All of us need more manpower," Keb added. I opened my mouth, yearning to refute the claim, but Timothy wrapped his arm around me to lead me back to my room. The book was not in my hand anymore. It was better left with them. Who knew what could happen in twenty years.

"So, Timothy," I whispered, "you're good at knowing your way around here."

"I memorized the entire map. It's not that hard," he replied. "Also, your keycard fell from your pocket when you were getting knocked over by that scum security."

"Can I have it back?"

"No," he hissed, holding his pistol in hand. I didn't have a sparing chance of taking my keycard from him. I simply had to play along with the game.

"Can you promise me that you won't choke me awake in twenty years?" I asked.

"I have no other way of waking you up from the inside, other than hacking the preservation system to make you suffocate," he replied.

"Well," I fabricated a smile, "I look forward to the next meeting."

"We will anticipate the last with our lives," he said. "We will be done recruiting, and we will start getting reckless when our new home is in sight."

He had that evil laugh you would only hear from a fictional villain. I assumed it was in my best interest to keep silent.

CHAPTER
NINETEEN

I woke again to the thick gasses, choking me to cautiousness. This time, however, I knew exactly where to hit my hand.

Whoosh! I gasped for air; my lungs throbbed. Every time I attempted to take a full breath, the pain would only get worse.

"This isn't fun, you know," I informed the dark silhouette beside me. Timothy's rough hand grabbed mine and pulled me to my feet.

"I know, but that is how we all wake each other up," he whispered. I kept on choking out the itch from my throat, but it didn't seem to sooth the itch. Every one of my coughs pushed out a thick muck from my lungs.

"Are you okay, buddy?" he said.

"I'm fine." I managed not to puke the mixture that sat in my stomach for two decades. Thinking about time, I looked at the clock above.

Minute: 47
Hour: 10
Day: 30
Week: 4

Finally, the trip was approaching the end. Thirteen more hours, and we would be arriving in Tau. I coughed a final time; the muck was on my tongue. Part of it must have been mucus and the other part, a sour gas. I never realized how sour it was until I really drank it. The irritation in my stomach faded away.

"What's the game plan?" I asked, subtly wishing I was not in the position to act.

"Well, I don't want to spoil the game," he whispered. I shivered at either the raspy sound of his voice or the collage of words. Whatever it must have been, it didn't sound right. I placed my hand on his shoulders, and he led me through the dark halls. It was still a little hard to swallow the truth of his team wanting me dead.

Questions rose to the tip of my tongue, but as my Grandpa once told me, 'curiosity kills.'

We continued to walk to the same location of our last meeting without a peep. The memory of the path's direction was still fresh in my mind. This spaceship had so many compartments, the designers must have been against the state themselves. They must have known where the prime meeting spots were.

After two minutes of pacing through the halls, a dull illumination came from ahead. Whispers polluted the air, disclosing a congregation much larger than the first time I was there. About fifty people stopped to watch us walk into the room. They had every right to be defensive. It was too dark to assume everyone was a human.

Nice to meet you again, Storm." Keb turned around, standing beside one of the only sources of light.

"Nice to see you again, too." I was quick to respond. It was twenty years since our last meeting, but it only seemed like ten minutes ago. Someone wrapped themselves around me from behind. Startled, I jumped and turned around.

"Great minds think alike." Theo's recognizable face was pressed against my chest.

"Theo," I whispered, squeezing him back. His presence wasn't helpful; I wanted him far from conflict. "Why are you here?"

"I hate Jem, and we need to take her down," he replied, still hugging me. It was almost burdensome to watch over myself, let alone another. Keb smirked, but he seemed to be in a hurry to carry out his operation.

"This takeover will be swift. It should not take any longer than thirty minutes. We have communicated with other Neo-Revolutionaries in the neighboring ships, and we have all planned on the exact moment of attack." He turned his wrist to observe the backside of his hand, revealing a classically styled watch. I was not sure if I should have been astonished by the fact that it was functioning after a century.

"Again, this should be swift," he said. I smiled, agreeing. Over one hundred cyborgs were ready to sacrifice themselves, and we had roughly fifty people, many of whom did not want death. Keb continued to speak. "We are going to blast a hole on every robot on this ship, and half of the ship's populace would sympathize, maybe join."

"What about Jem, the captain?" I asked, hesitant.

"Like I said last time, she complies with us, or she's dead." Keb was transitioning back into a state of anger. He pulled out a pistol from his back pocket. Everyone else stood, following his lead. I stood frozen, not sure if my own safety was assured. For all that I knew, Keb was an unpredictable person. I couldn't be at rest when he held a gun.

"Storm, will you join us?" he asked. I opened my mouth, thinking of a response. I didn't want to fight, but the thought of a mother and her sacrifice made me think rash. If I fought for a cause, I had to do it for a reason. From what I saw, the Neo-Revolutionaries wanted to preserve freedom and life, Pangaea did not.

"I'm not good with guns," I said, unable to think of a clever escape. "I never shot one in my life."

"Then you will learn today." He handed his pistol to me. I toyed with it until the trigger was on my finger. It was cold and heavy with the black metal coating. He also pulled two loaded clips from the back of his pocket for me. They must have had little trouble smuggling such quantities of ammunition if it was passed around so freely.

"Is this the only type of weapon we have?" Theo caressed the pistol with his finger, observing its quality.

"When you boarded this ship, Cyborg Security would bellhop your luggage for you. While they held your luggage, they would scan it for weapons or explosives without you noticing it. As Neo-Revolutionaries, we had to find the loophole in the system. Timothy, I, and several others brought 3D printer parts with metal ink. Our team assembled the printer in my preservation room, but we did not have enough ink for larger weaponry. So, we had to resort to printing smaller guns."

"That's awesome!" Theo bounced, inspecting the pistol. It was smooth to the touch. I would have never believed it was printed. One shot to the motherboard of the cyborg was one shot to its brain. I grabbed Keb's shoulder before he could have turned around and addressed the crowd of Neo-Revolutionaries, most of whom seemed far beyond prepared to win a fight.

"Do we really have a chance of winning this?" I placed my other hand on Theo. Keb met eyes with me and stepped closer. He was only three inches away from my face. We were sharing the same air.

"We can do this, okay?" he said.

I felt warm breaths brush my nose. I didn't want to question him further as there was no turning back. I joined the revolutionaries in a rash decision. I had to finish what I started. He turned around to the crowd of bloodthirsty soldiers. I brought my lips to Theo's ear.

"What are you planning to do when this operation begins?" I asked. He looked up and inched closer to me.

"I am going to shoot Jem in the face for what she did in Niamey."

I paused, struck by the fact that he would say something like that. The Theo I knew was kind and energetic; he was not resentful and bloodthirsty.

"Well, she's the reason why we are here and not dead on Earth."

"Storm, we don't even know if the nuclear war that she was talking about even happened. Jem is a lying snake, and you know that too."

"Anyone can be a liar, even me."

"But I've known you for sixteen years," he said, pulling away from me as I looked into his grey, sorrowful eyes. I leaned in for a final time.

"I love you, Theo. Don't do something that you don't want to do. You're not being the Theo I know." I cradled his soft face with my hands and leaned in to kiss his forehead. My lips sparked, magnetized to him. Maybe he knew now about the way I felt for him. He didn't seem fazed by it. I looked down.

"Fellow comrades," Keb began. "In a little bit, we need to begin taking our places. We are aware that motion sensors are placed throughout the ship, so we need to begin by maneuvering around them."

I gritted my teeth at the sound of his plan. It was risky, but it had to be done. If no one did it, we would end up as slaves of a supercomputer for the rest of our lives.

"Our best bet is to begin by taking over the third floor," he said. "We will have the leverage of height, so we can secure the stairwells. Anything that goes up will be shot back down to the bottom of the stairwell." Other nodded their heads like they heard this plan before.

"Smash them!" Timothy clenched his fists. Despite the fear, their silent energy was the propulsion I needed to remain optimistic. Keb must have felt the passion, and he inflated his chest.

"They should obey us, not fight us because we created them!" Keb was no longer silent, piercing sound around us. "If they do not obey, then we will make sure that they turn into the material that we used to build them!" He scanned the energized army, reading their red faces. He returned to a soft tone, right before I felt poked by the uncomforted. "We are going to win this because we have something that they don't: a conscious."

I was unnoticeably nodding. What he said was right. Humans were not going to abide by computers anymore. It killed the mother I didn't get to know, and I was not going to let it kill me. It was time to take back what belonged to us. It was my shot for true vengeance.

CHAPTER TWENTY

The pistol was no longer cold as it rested in the warm embrace of my hand. Holding it became second nature.

"Yellow speaking; Magenta in?" a muffled voice came from Keb's pocket.

"Magenta in. Black in?"

He lifted his portable radio in the dead-silent room and clicked a button on its side.

"Black in, five minutes," Keb said. The exchange was only several seconds long. Maybe it was because the batteries limited it from any casual gossip. Keb clipped the radio onto the side of his pocket, letting it bulge out.

With a pistol latched onto one side and radio on the other, he seemed more like a police officer than a soldier. Everyone else seemed like armed civilians. Most of them held their pistols like an action movie star. They were like me: inexperienced with more fury than ammunition.

"Everyone split into two groups. One will be led by Timothy, and the other will be led by me," Keb said. I stepped beside him. Theo followed me.

Adrenaline was already kicking in my veins. Keb took my hand and placed it on his shoulder. Theo has his hand on mine, and we moved forward in the darkness.

I clenched the pistol to my chest. Keb paced carefully and paused several times for the group to catch up. No one dared to speak, not even the leader. We were maneuvering through the halls like lost children. I sensed Keb turning his head around, and the seal between his lips broke open.

"Watch your feet. The stairs begin here. Pass it on," he said. I turned to Theo and repeated the words. Keb kept walking forward. The sounds of his boots on stairs gave away a squeal. I moved forward to take a leap of faith. My foot landed on the escalated stair. I could no longer hear the footsteps of the other group; maybe they left to occupy the other end of the stairwell, so very far away. My feet moved up the stairs with grace. That was only until I heard someone grunt.

Bang! A flash lit up the staircase, and the noise rang in my ears. Instead of holding my ears from the ringing, I turned around, substituted the stair as a seat, and pointed my gun ahead. My hand pressed the trigger, seeing nothing ahead. The gunfire sounded forced, so we couldn't give it a fighting chance. I squeezed the trigger, and a growing sense of uncertainty squeezed it further. My breath slowed down to a halt. A wave of calm washed over me.

"I tripped, it was a mistake!" someone shouted. "Is everyone okay?"

The lights above shot on without warning. My gun was pointed at Theo's chest. Shock froze him in place.

"Storm," he trembled. I immediately let go of the trigger. Sweat trickled from my forehead.

"We need to go up, now!" Keb shouted, pushing the persistent ring in my ear. I launched myself forward, and so did everyone else. We darted up the linear staircase without thinking. Theo bounced up the stairs ahead of the crowd. It was no longer a uniform group; it was every man for himself.

"Passengers, we have most, unfortunately, came across another lockdown," Jem's voice beamed from the speakers above. *"Please lock your doors immediately."* Her voice shook in the end, knowing exactly what was occurring on her ship.

We approached the end of the staircase. All of it was too foreign to me. Theo and Keb knew the environment better than most of us.

"Get ready!" Keb barked, out of breath; his throat squealed. Every floor had an identical main hall, housing hundreds of preservation rooms. In the depth of the distance, comrades from Timothy's group seemed like they already held the position. Some were lying on their belly. Others leaned beside the stairwell entrance for cover. I threw myself into a nearby wall, covering myself from potential gunfire.

Two groups, two stairwells, and the third floor was ours to defend. Theo fell flat on the floor. His head peeked below towards the empty stairwell. For a moment, it seemed like he forgot I existed. He didn't bother to scan the soldiers who stood beside him, let alone his best friend.

For a final time, I shot a glimpse of the eerie stairwell. I kept my back pressed against the cover behind me: the only barrier between life and death. I was not going to let an atom of space divide me from the wall behind. All I could hear was deep breaths and footsteps. These footsteps came from below, and I was certain that they did not belong to human feet.

CHAPTER
TWENTY-ONE

The rasp bangs of bullets came echoing across the hall. Timothy's group already met opposition. Their guns pointed down, but the bullets pierced my courage.

Suddenly, Theo began to fire. He shot blindly as others aimed ahead. They were making a foolhardy risk by exposing their heads; but then, we were fighting an enemy that didn't process fear.

Bullets clinked on metal, clearly the cyborgs. There was no response from the bottom of the staircase. I replicated the brave and peeked into the stairwell, witnessing three cyborgs attempting to climb over the corpses of other security bots. Their masks covered their metal identity. A part of me wanted to know what was under them. It may just be a collage of wires.

I threw my hands into the hallway, clenching the pistol's trigger. My hands jerked back with every shot.

Bang! Bang! Bang! I threw myself back beside the wall. I thought I hit one of the cyborgs, but I wasn't quite sure. This wasn't like the movies where you simply had to blast away your enemies. Bullets began to fling back, digging into the wall behind us.

Cowardice kept me planted behind the wall, waiting for the gunfire to come to a halt. Theo clicked his hollow pistol. He remained to lie on the floor, drawing a fresh clip from his pocket. I never saw him fire a gun prior to this moment, but he seemed to have experience with it. I was certain it was the videogames.

"Storm, take my place!" Keb barked, running to the other side of the hallway. He was in the middle of gunfire, but it didn't seem to faze him. I stepped to his spot and ducked, hiding behind a large man for cover. In a display of courage, my legs pushed the ground below me. I was standing, pointing my gun at two cyborgs who attempted to run up the stairs. I shot twice, only to squat down again. This time, however, I heard the bullet clink of metal. I was too terrified to witness its effect. Cheers from the other side of the halls distracted me.

"What is going on?" I asked the soldier beside me. He didn't bother replying as he shot several rounds ahead.
Gradually, silence filled the halls. I looked ahead to see a pile of lifeless cyborgs.

"We did it!" Theo cried.

"Yes!" another shouted. From the looks of it, only ten were truly shot dead. The celebration was premature, and I held my gun tighter than before. Theo stood, hugging me.

"It's not over," I whispered, locking eyes with him.

"What do you mean?" he said. The lights were swift to close, revealing nothing but silence.

"Do you think you will win this?" Jem's voice was patronizing as always. *"Lay down your weapons or face the consequence."*

"We need to come with a plan, now!" I said; my frantic heart pounded. Cyborgs had night vision. We were just dead men standing in pitch black. Bickering from the other side of the dark halls seeped into ours, panic weaving amongst ourselves. I would look like a coward if I were the only one to drop my gun.

"Stop!" Theo barked. I heard light footsteps from the second level. "All third-floor preservation rooms have windows. If we open all the doors and windows, we have light!"

"Good plan!" Someone shouted from the other side of the hall. I felt the wall beside me. It was the only map I needed to maneuver.

"I will go door to door," I insisted, keeping the strongest on the frontlines. As for Theo, I silently prayed that he remained far from gunfire. My hand felt a wooden door. I knocked frantically and conveyed a message that would reach as many people as I could meet.

"Open your door and window," I hesitated, "for the revolution!"

I repeated myself like a broken record player. The clatter of gunfire approached closer until I felt the vibrations of the ruptures on my chest. Shouting was only a background noise, and the panic commenced.

I failed to hear Theo's voice in the commotion. I began to approach a quarter way through the hall, and the only way I could tell was from the sound itself.

The words spewing from my mouth didn't process anymore. As I stopped from one door to the next, the collage of sound came out as a pattern of sound.

"Open your door and window for the revolution."
"Open your door and window for the revolution."
"Open your door and window for the revolution."

Bullet shots began to ring from all directions with no light in sight. I slouched beside the wall and held my hands to my head.

"I'm sorry Grandpa," I whispered, looking above with the darkness swallowing me whole. Everything was lost and gone. A gradual glimmer of light caught my attention.

One door opened with a light brighter than I had witnessed since Earth. Maybe we already approached the Tau's solar system. I ducked, darting towards the room. A young woman stood beside the door, and her face was full of fear. She opened her eyes to the pistol in my hand, keeping her hands in the air.

This was my only chance to seek asylum in a closing warzone. Sounds of bullets were flinging across the halls. It was as if the Neo-Revolutionaries were firing at each other. I could have stepped into the hallway, but that was a risk that would kill me without a doubt. More doors began to creak open, filling the floor with a warm light.

"Stay away from the halls," Keb shouted to onlookers, all watching in terror. The light was a radiating hope that caressed my heart. I waited for my moment, but the longer I waited, an urge to step into the gunfire grew. I scanned both sides of the hallway. Some were throwing punches, some lied on the floor, and others were covered in blood.

If I had to die taking the risk to prove myself to Grandpa, stand up for Theo, seek vengeance for my mother, I had to act fast. I let anger fuel me. Time seemed to have slowed down. Keb struggled to hold a cyborg down, most likely out of bullets. I darted towards the masked metal man and held my hardly used pistol to its head.

Bang! It slumped to the ground, and Keb threw it to the side. Without hesitation, I darted forward, to a cyborg that lifted its gun towards one of the comrades.

Before the piece of metal could have laid a finger on the trigger, I pointed my pistol at its head, letting it feel my fury.

Somehow, I slipped into the stairwell without a scratch. Maybe Grandpa was watching me from above, proud that I truly fought for what was right.

In a flash, a cyborg turned the corner, frozen like me. Before it barbed its pistol towards me, I squeezed my finger, pointing it towards its head.

Bang! It fell onto the floor; the last shot I heard. It was finally tranquil; I was finally able to hear my shaky breath. Cheers rocked the third floor again. This time, it was fueled by onlooking passengers. For the first time in a long time, I was smiling.

"Let's keep moving!" I shouted with a red face. Nobody followed suit because they were looking down on their fallen soldiers. I rushed up the stairs to feel my stomach turn. Some were wounded, but others were suffocated in a pool of their own blood.

Unfamiliar faces bumped past me, tending the wounded. Some passengers began to pull the pistols from lifeless cyborgs to use for themselves. I frantically looked for Theo. Regret was pooling over me for every second I failed to find him.

"Theo!" I shouted, attempting to hear a reply. I felt a hand grab onto my ankle. I glanced at the man in black. He was not Theo, but he was lying with a lost face. He had punctures in his stomach.

"Don't worry." I began to shake. "I'll help you."

"No," he struggled to speak; his blue eyes locked onto mine.

"What? No?" I smiled with the help of hysteria. "I'll patch you up."

"Tell my lover..."

"No, I'll get you fixed up." I grabbed a rag that lied on the floor. It must have belonged to Keb, who kept running back and forth. My hand lifted the man's black shirt, revealing two bullet wounds. Blood seeped out of his wounds and onto the black carpeting.

"Sir, you'll be fine by the ti-" I tried to place the cloth on his messy wounds, but his blue eyes were looking at the ceiling. He didn't blink, once.

"Oh dear," I stepped back, running into Keb, looking blindly at the man.

"Kevin!" he cried, "oh, my Kevin!"

A quarter of the team lied dead, another quarter: injured. It was now up to a few of us to continue the battle. Theo must have been in his room; it was only across the hall. I would rather have him safe than sorry. That thought was short to live.

"Hey, Storm." Jem was almost excited to speak. *"Looks like I have your friend here, Theo? Yes, that is what his name is. Now, I know you care for him dearly. It would be such a shame if something happened to him."* She ended her message with dry laughs and Theo's muffled screams.

"No!" I shouted, stomping my foot. The grip on my pistol was so tight, it could have fired a bullet into the floor. They must have taken him when the lights were off. I should have done more to protect him; it was all my fault.

"Did I hear something?" Jem said. She heard every word, maybe watching over us as well.

"Stop it," I shouted. A louder part of me wanted to strangle her dead. "Stop this or you're going to die."

"Oh honey, not if your little friend dies first," she replied. I looked around frantically, but everyone was tending the wounded. Even Keb was mourning his loss. The thought of mother appeared. Her effort for peace pushed forward despite popular belief. Bullets were not going to solve the conflict anymore. Jem believed in dialogue, and so it may work.

"We want to make a truce!" I said.

"Then drop your gun and make your way down here." She was quick to respond. Almost everyone stopped to watch me. I met eyes with Keb, and I saw the tears come down his face. He nodded, and I nodded back. My pistol fell to the floor with unused clip. It was time to make peace.

CHAPTER
TWENTY-TWO

As I stepped down the stairwell, the lights flicked on again. A lingering scent of burnt metal brushed against my nose. It counteracted the stench of death.

Unknowingly, my hands were raised. Blood that did not belong to me stained the palm of my right hand. I approached the second floor. It was quiet, too quiet. And I found it hard to believe that all the cyborgs were shot into bits.

"This is Storm Raleston," my voice trembled, bearing an undertone of uncertainty. "I am here to make peace."

I stepped closer to the corner of the stairwell and waved my hand out the corner. In return, I received the response of dead silence. I shook myself loose and took a deep breath. Cyborgs were no longer the enemy: fear was.

My head peeked out from the corner to observe several cyborgs pointing their guns in my direction. I was either walking into a firing squad or the first steps to saving Theo's life. I stepped into range of potential gunfire. My chest was close to bursting.

"You are Storm Raleston?" one of the masked security cyborgs asked. Its monotone voice sent a chill down my spine.

"Yes," I said, "and I'm here to make a truce."

Some were on a knee, and others stood. I would hope that they would escort me, but that was not the case. I was aware that I had to stay far from moving, stepping, or even breathing out of place.

All they did was observe my every move with caution. I moved back into the stairwell for the first level. Cyborgs lined up on every step. This was a battle that we were not going to win, peace deal or not. There were simply too many of them left. I stepped past every creviced stair.

Although my legs were trembling, my feet had a solid grip. I heard the faint sounds of commotion from two floors above, distinctly Keb. He screamed in agony. My lunges were breathing fire; my heart pounded relentlessly. The cyborgs were dead stiff.

Perhaps Jem was manually holding over their shells. Whatever it was, I kept my gaze low, submissive to the overwhelming force I passed by. I made it to the ground level without hyperventilating. I turned the corner to see five cyborgs move towards me.

"I am Storm Raleston," I reminded. Unfortunately, that didn't stop them. Two approached me from the side and clenched me from my arms. I was finally able to put down my arms, worn from tension.

"We are going to take you to Jem Hata," the one on my left replied. I thought of a crippling remark, but Theo's life was far more important to me. I had to refrain from saying anything that hindered the process. As we passed every door, including mine, I noticed how eerie silent the spaceship was. We were the only houses of life for quadrillions of miles, and everyone fearfully huddled in their rooms for protection. They were not protected if the spaceship was amid a revolution, let alone a deadly one.

I was lost in the thought of safety, and the hallway zoomed to an end, freezing my breath once more. I couldn't feel my legs, and Jem was holding the only one I cared for in a death grip.

Swoosh! The revealing door opened to the spacious cabin. I darted my eyes around the room and caught a glimpse of Theo, strapped onto a seat, lathered in tape. His plush cheeks tried to push out from the harsh grip of it. Jem lifted her chin, pressing a pistol towards Theo's head. She remained tall with the help of malevolency. I tried to rush up to Theo, but the security cyborg's grip on my arms was an immobile one.

"Jem, we want to end this conflict just as much as you do," I pleaded, almost tripping on myself. She moved her eyes towards me, keeping the pistol on

Theo's head. I couldn't bear to watch it. His eyes were closed, and his hair shook.

"Do you really think I can just let you off the hook?" she responded. I continued to step closer to her until we were just several feet apart. The windows displayed the magenta and yellow spaceships, gliding with tranquility around a vibrant blue and green sphere. We were in Tau's orbit, but no one dared to land as far as I could have told.

Maybe we were losing the battle in one ship, winning in the other. Tau's atmosphere was the only thing blanketing the image on the windows. It did look like a replicated Earth without the tainted tattoos of humankind.

"Look at that." I pointed to the display, attempting to ease tension. "Doesn't that view put you in awe?"

"Yeah, it does." Jem began to loosen her stiffened posture. She looked at the clean planet. If we agreed on something, then we had a foundation for peace. But I knew deep down inside that she was smarter than that. Her rough grasp pressed the pistol with more force to Theo's ear, crocking his head to the side. I held my hand in the air.

"Look," I spoke with a fabricated calm, "we need to talk first, can we?"

"Yes," she said, "it requires one thing tha-"

She was interrupted by muffled sounds that came from the control panel. She turned her wide eyes to the side for a second, but she returned them back to me. The muffles seemed to be a human voice, frantic and panicked. Suddenly, the incomprehensible shouting and pleas stopped. A glimmer from the window caught my eye. The magenta spaceship was all too far away, but it began to split into several directions. Like a slowed explosion, fragments continued to break, some hurdling into the Tau atmosphere. I kept my mouth open, unknowingly shaking my head at the horror. Jem must have caught along, gazing out the window.

"This is what you have caused!" She motioned to me with her pistol, almost making me believe I would be shot first. Instead, she pounced it on Theo's head; he grunted.

"No." I held out my hand again. "Look, just tell me what you want for a truce."

She pressed her hand on the radio, leaning into it. If two security men weren't standing beside me, I would have moved closer to her. I could have knocked the pistol from her hand and held her in place.

"Mosad, do you copy?" she shook, waiting for several long seconds. Then, a loud, almost painful grunt came from her. Her face was riddled with uncertainty. "I am not going to get harmed by this conflict."

"No, you will not be harmed." I looked at her squint, blinding her brown eyes. "I can promise that if we can make sure that Theo goes unharmed too."

A third of what remains of the human population had perished. We were the pockets of what was left, and the thought of that made me fear death less.

"Okay, then it looks like we have a deal." She nodded. Her control panel began to beep. It sounded far from assuring. A red light glimmered with caution, and sweat began to trickle down her face.

"What is going on?" I questioned.

"It looks like your friends decided to move to the second floor," she hissed. The security in the cabin darted for the door. They left the three of us to watch each other in silence.

"This was not the plan," I shook. "Like I said, I will make sure that you're left *unharmed*."

Her purple afro began to droop as her eyeshadow smeared. She seemed more uncertain and petrified than me. A tear began to roll down her cheek. Shame was traveling into every inch of my body. Jem was not an enemy. She simply wanted peace, like me. She was the only one on board this mission that knew my mother.

Despite her secretive character, she seemed to have cared for us. Jem was the one who supplied the secret medicine to make us perfect candidates for this mission. She spared my life for holding revolutionary propaganda; she was anything but an enemy.

"I'm so sorry." I gazed at the floor below, too ashamed to look up.

"This is how I am replayed after I saved your life?" Tears were flowing from her eyes. It was betrayal, and I was guilty.

"But, what about the book?" I pointed to the bookshelf. "It says that Earth was destroyed by Pangaea after we left."

"That," she emphasized, her face inflated, "is true, but that wasn't in my power."

She lied to Grandpa and Theo's parents. Nuclear warfare was not the problem; it was nuclear genocide, and every inch of Earth was left in a blazing fire. She knew this entire time, but she lied. It was hard to believe that any human being would do such a thing.

I didn't know what to feel. I didn't know if I had to feel ashamed or angered. Thump after thump, the door behind me interrupted my thoughts. The Neo-Revolutionaries arrived.

CHAPTER
TWENTY-THREE

I knew that this was a recipe for disaster, so I had to act to prevent toxicity from adding to the situation. Pounding on the door failed to end. I heard Keb's distinguishable shouts from the other side.

"We made a deal!" I barked, hoping that it would quell the noise. Unfortunately, Keb and his team kept howling and barging on the thick metal door. It was beyond my comprehension that they made it past all the cyborgs in such short time.

No one was in his or her right conscience, and time was needed to blend the lines between peace and bloodshed. Theo was glaring at me like I was the rope that would lift him out. His life was not in Jem's hands, but mine. I had to make this right.

"Stop shouting!" I screeched. This time, it began to quell. It seemed like ten men were behind the door, but that only made me wonder what happened to the rest. Their shouts muffled into whispers as if they were planning something cunning. I glanced back at Jem, who began to un-tape Theo's mouth.

"Tell him you want to live!" She motioned to me with her gun, causing me to flinch.

"Storm, please." Theo shook, sounding like he was already roughed up from his tone. His lips were red from the hard-pressed tape. My eyes began to moisten. I couldn't bear to look at his trembling hands, attempting to shake away from the tape that bonded his arms to the armrest.

"Open this door!" Keb barked from the other side.

"Wait!" I moved towards the metal door. I didn't bother to think that bullets could pierce its fabric. "Theo is being held hostage, and we already made a deal!"

"Deal is off!" Keb replied. Jem shook her head and pressed her pistol right behind Theo's head. She began to squeeze the trigger.

"It's not!" I said. "No, the deal is not off!" I waited for Keb to reply from the halls, but all that came through were unrecognizable whispers.

"How does the deal go?" he asked.

"Jem gets to live if Theo does." I began to shake to the point where my stomach felt sick, feeling the burden latch onto my shoulders to drag me down. Keb grunted, but he seemed to have leaned closer to the door.

"I'll work with that," he said.

"Are you sure?" I asked.

"Yeah, I'm sure."

I didn't know if I could have trusted it. But I had to take the leap of faith. Jem was no longer speaking, letting Theo's fear speak for her.

"I only expect one of you to come in!" I yelled, subtly hoping that they took the message to heart.

"Storm," Jem interrupted me, "I see them on camera. Tell the other twelve to back away." That must have meant that there were thirteen in total, and Keb was one of them. The others were probably dead. She was jerking her head to the control panel that I couldn't see.

"Keb, tell your soldiers to take ten steps back!" I shouted. "Also, drop your gun." More silent muffles came from the lifeless hallway until it became pitch silent again.

"Done," he said. Jem kept her head turned the entire time, watching from the display.

"They backed away, and he dropped his gun." She seemed determined, but anxiety bit her upper lip.

"Okay," I assured, "you can come in." I looked back to Jem, hoping that she would control the door. Instead, she motioned her gun towards the button beside me. I leaped over and held my hand over the blue button. She trusted me to open and close the door, yet I couldn't trust myself.

Click! The door drew up to Keb strolling all too casually into the spacious cabin. Blood trickled down his neck; it was a fresh cut. The others lined up behind him, observing me. Some had fresh wounds while others seemed unscathed. Behind them, a pile of cyborgs lied on top of each other.

It was true; we did win the battle. My hand flinched towards the button again, and the door began to close on itself. Keb had a smirk on his face.

"I see that we have made a peace deal." He drew a smirk from the corners of his lips. It didn't look right. Before I had to answer, Jem replied impatiently.

"Yes," she said. A smear of black mascara dried on her dark face, forming a cracked appearance.

"We need to spare her life if we want Theo alive," I pleaded, but that didn't seem to convince him. "He was fighting with us."

"Hm," he pondered aloud, trialing around the limited floor space. He gave distance to the two by the control panel. "I don't see why I would want that purple-haired bitch to be alive."

Jem began to clench her loosely hanging hand.

"Don't shoot him!" I pleaded. "We will keep you alive!" I felt like I ran a marathon. Sweat poured out of me. Theo gritted his glistening teeth together, petrified beyond my imagination.

"No." Keb kneeled, his hands petting his tall boots, almost like he was rushed to do so. I didn't know what he was doing until I observed a lump in the right boot. It was too noticeable; a small pistol was tugged in his boot. His right hand began to glide carefully to it.

"Don't," I whispered, shaking my already quivering head. I felt like I was whispering to myself. "Please, don't."

Suddenly, he dug into his boot and pulled out the small gun. It was the size of a hummingbird. Jem clenched the trigger further, stepping closer to Theo. I chomped on my lip, almost tasting blood.

"Don't do this, Keb!" I said again, feeling the power drain from my fingertips. He began to squint, aiming directly at Jem. I could knock the pistol from his hand, but that kind of rashness would've only trigged Jem. We were all frozen. No one dared to move a muscle. I opened my mouth, trying to let any dialogue pour from it.

"You know, Storm," Jem sounded calm, "I am quite saddened that it ha-"

Bang! Keb's gun lit up, and a trail of steam followed. I stopped hearing, feeling, breathing. I glanced at Theo first. His eyes were closed, but he seemed unmarked. I finally observed Jem. She had a hole in her forehead, but nothing came out; that only meant one thing. Her eyes began to roll back, but her finger began to pull the trigger. Theo seemed so calm, almost happy. His blue eyebrows curved. I had to run. Theo was in the firing range.

"Theo!" I shouted, taking one giant leap to the next. He must have thought I was running to hug him. He was far from right. I had to push him from Jem's tightly clenching hand. The pistol was only three inches away from his scalp, and I was only several strides away, leaping with every inch of muscle that mother had given me. My hands touched his seat rest, warm and plush. We were getting out of this, without a doubt.

Bang! I jerked back and watched Theo's seat fall to the side. His grey eyes shut halfway, gracefully falling. I almost tripped over his seat as I pushed him aside. But he lied there, not moving a muscle. Jem fell to the ground with a silver hole in her forehead. Perhaps he was no longer conscience from the fall. It wasn't until an engraining image caught my eye. The bullet already pierced his frail skull.

"Theo!" I couldn't feel myself, losing every sensing nerve in my body. "Wake up, Theo. Don't do this to me!"

I leaned beside him; he was still strapped to the chair. Anything that came out of my mouth must have been gibberish. I tried to shake him, but he wobbled in the seat. He must have just been unconscious; he had to respond to me. Blood poured onto the floor.

"Theo!" I barked again; my face began to boil. My uncontrollable hands shook him again, but no

response came. He looked like he was sleeping. Every shake flopped around his tangerine hair.
Keb said something, but I couldn't hear it. Tears began to force out of my eyes.

"He's dead, buddy," Keb repeated himself, but I was not going to take it.

"No, he's not!" I barked.

"He is, and he's not coming back," he assured. I couldn't see, choking on the idea of losing the one I cared for most. I *loved* him. I loved him all my life, and he never knew it. He was gone.

Dead.

CHAPTER
TWENTY-FOUR

My hands were unconsciously unraveling the multiple layers of tape that cuffed Theo. A growing pool of blood made me feel sick. Tears pushed themselves out, landing on the soft mesh of his shirt. I couldn't find myself to accept his fate, but reality sanctioned the thought.

He was gone. I had no one left. I had nothing to live for. I had nothing to lose. Keb slowly walked towards the door like his business was done. He was not done. He was the reason why Theo died, and justice had to be served. Jem's pistol lied a foot away from her hand, frozen in time.

"This is for you, Theo," I choked, hardly able to let the words loose. I lurched towards the gun beside her, attempting to stabilize its heavy weight in my hand.

"Hey," my numb lips trembled. It was like I was under an earthquake, hardly able to hold my balance. Keb ignored my call, continuing to stroll towards the door. I barbed the pistol towards him and began to fire several shots. Some hit him, others missed. He slouched to the ground. I didn't even hear the gunshots. The thoughts in my head were far more amplified. My legs wobbled back onto the ground, piercing my knees with a sharp pain. I began to weep, hardly able to breathe.

I let my head lie on Theo's chest. He looked like he was sleeping. tranquil and silent. He seemed to have a small grin on his pink lips. I wanted to stop breathing. I was a split second away from saving his life, but I failed.

I failed. I failed. I failed. My eyes locked gaze with the pistol that was grasped tightly in my hand. I had to face the consequence of failing Mother, Grandpa, and Theo. I failed myself and pulling a single trigger would end it all. It would end the pain that kept seeping from my moist eyes. It must have been a rash decision, but it would be relatively painless. I couldn't bear to live the rest of my life knowing that he could have been alive. He was my heart, and it was not beating without him.

Rash pounding on the door caught my attention. I tried to ignore it. Too many were dead over a conflict that I had no control over.

"Open this door!" a recognizable voice shouted. I attempted to stand, too weak and torn. The control panel flashed many colors. It was all foreign to me. Some buttons were flashing red as others blinked blue and green. A screen displayed the security cameras that scattered across the ship. Timothy pressed his weight on the door that separated me from the halls: the door between life and death. His hand was pounding on the door, and the others huddled around him. What if they saw their president lying dead? What would they make of it?

Through the window, I saw yellow spaceship glide towards Tau's atmosphere with grace. I didn't know what button to press.

"Open this damn door now!" Timothy fired several bullets into the door; it hardly budged. The firing sounded muffled form the other side, and so did their growing voices.

"Okay!" I rushed, feeling my senses restore. However, every time I glanced at Theo's lifeless body, I would go numb again. My stomach was trying to push out what was inside, but nothing came out.

"Where's Keb?" Timothy barked.

I wobbled towards Keb; his miniature pistol lied in his hand. Several bullets riddled his back. I didn't bother to flip him over. Instead, I plucked the miniature pistol from him.

"Yellow ship is occupied. We're landing, copy?" his radio said. I wanted to snatch the radio from his back pocket, but I let it sit there. *"Keb, do you copy?"*

I scurried towards the door and threw my hand at the door's button. It drew open to the twelve people. The pistol in my hand was clenched tightly, feeling every sharp crevice in its metal frame.

"Where is he?" Timothy stepped into the cabin, only locking eyes with me. I motioned to the lifeless body that lied several feet away. Timothy's face began to turn red, although it already was from the bruises. The other eleven observed his body and, they turned to me for answers.

"Who did it?" he asked. His scruffy facial hair seemed like it grew an inch from the last time I saw him. I didn't notice that everyone's weapons were pointing in my direction. I was either going to live or die. Both options were undesirable.

"I," I began to think quicker than usual, "I was standing by Keb, and..."

"...and what?" Timothy's body got bigger with every step he took towards me.

"Jem shot him." I dropped the pistol. Tears began to seep from my eyes as he got closer. "She also killed Theo, so I had to kill her myself." I waited for them to back away, but they continued to get closer. Pistols began to point towards the floor. A void of cluelessness blanketed their faces.

"But..." Timothy swallowed the following words.

"Before he passed..." I said; more tears came from my eyes, but they weren't for Keb. "He told me to lead the revolution for him."

They began to whisper to each other; a jury began to determine my fate. Cowardice kept me from telling the truth. They all nodded, agreeing amongst the whispers. I didn't bother to hear it. Instead, I gazed at Theo's body. We used to play tag as small children, innocent and ignorant. I always pictured us growing old together. It was all a fading fantasy.

"Well, you shot her…you're the hero." A smile formed on Timothy's face. He moved his hand down my arm and grasped my hand. I couldn't feel it. Maybe he was going to strangle me to death for failing to protect Keb. I felt my perception spin with every passing second. My hand was far beyond pale and dead. I began to quiver, silently praying that I was killed swiftly. Despite my pleas, Timothy threw my hand over my head.

"We will be glad to call you our temporary president. We will hold elections in two Tau years. Your powers ar-" his words were cut short because they flew around. I stumbled to the ground, collapsing.

I was shaking as I tried to lift myself off the marble floor. I was in the same spot, hoping that it was all a dream. Unfortunately, it was a reality. It felt like I just woke up, but it must have only been a few minutes. The door was sealed shut, but two men stayed beside me. Their backs were turned against me.

"Just press that button, and we will be going to the right anchor point!" someone shouted. The window displayed a blue sky and serene, green land.

"Where are we?" I tried to speak but couldn't hear myself. Everything was rattling, including me. The only rational guess was that we were already breaking through Tau's atmosphere. I struggled to find my feet in the unstable ship. My hands brushed past the two guards beside me.

"Please, stay down, Mr. Raleston!" persuaded a thin soldier. His eyes were restless and moist, but it didn't make it worse than mine. I stripped Keb from his title, which was now plastered onto me. I was responsible for his death, and I was the only conscious person to know it.

Trees and mountains as far as the eye can see became closer to every passing second. Rivers and birds came to view. They were flying away, maybe even petrified. Some had horns, and others had beaks that were bigger than the ones seen on Earth.

"I've got it in control. We're going to be landing right by yellow in the habitable zone." the soldier beside the control panel said. Some were prematurely cheering as they saw the yellow ship come to sight. It was in a marsh, alongside lanky grass. Everything outside the windows had color, true vibrant color. But little did the life forms here know, an ugly virus arrived in two metal bodies.

We lowered onto the marsh, scuffing the grass right beside the yellow ship. I lurched forward, but I caught my balance before I fell.

"We landed!" Timothy shouted from the face of the cabin control panel, looking back towards me. He was cheering, as did everyone else.

Soldiers march forward despite the deaths of their comrades. Today, I was a soldier, a leader, a man. My eyes were dry because no more tears were left to spare.

CHAPTER
TWENTY-FIVE

An automated voice began to resonate from the ceiling. It sounded like Jem, making me cringe a little. It told us to take a medical and food supply pack, and leave the spaceship's premises. There was no sign of help or hope. We were on our own, a queue for natural selection to begin. The soldiers that fought so hard to overthrow Jem from the ship were now clueless. I didn't know most of their names, except for the fallen.

"How are we going to do this?" Timothy spoke with an undertone of uncertainty. One choice was all that was needed to succeed or fail. Fearlessness had to take the first steps.

"Let's get out," I insisted. No human had stepped foot on this planet. From the foreign nature of this it, the ground could've possibly swallowed us whole. I stepped by the microphone sticking from the control panel, and it automatically adjusted to level my chin.

"Good day to everyone," I tried to sound calm. "I am glad to announce that we have landed safely. Again, everyone must take one medical and preserved food kit."

I heard my own voice from the speakers above. It was delayed by half a second, sounding starkly different than what I heard in my head. Fear echoed from each word. I looked back at the fighters, watching over me. I shouldn't have to fear them any longer if they were going to be protecting me.

"You need to tell them about yourself." Timothy stepped closer. I cleared my throat.

"I am Storm Raleston, and I am the appointed leader." It was then that I realized Timothy was holding his radio right to my lips, let me announce to the neighboring ship. I had to harvest any inch of hope for us to move forward. "Many have died to overthrow a government responsible for the eradication of life on Earth. Many may not survive what is to come on this planet, but staying together is crucial for our survival. Today, we don't identify ourselves as loyalists or Neo-Revolutionists, but as human beings," I said.

I let the message end there as there was no more to say. Then I walked towards the wide-open exit to the halls. We had to go to the back of the ship, the only way to reach the outdoors. Hundreds began to seep out form their preservation rooms, uncertain yet hopeful.

Corpses of metal men stopped many in their tracks, but that didn't stop me from walking over them. Medical kits and dried food threw themselves from the ceiling; thin strands of string prevented them from breaking loose.

The hallway became thinner with every stride. I fabricated a smile to potential losses, and they smiled back. All of them looked similar. I was ready to get ingested in a lively, warm sun. I continued walking all the way to the end, past the seats in the back. I approached the sideways door, and I turned to the passengers who followed my lead to the new outside.

History class taught me that early humans hunted and gathered in packs. Many died in the process, but groups with stronger leaders prevailed. They would use their intelligence to their advantage.

From there, arose thriving civilizations, societies, and a destructive force that could kill thousands with the switch of a button. It was a malignant cycle, but that was what made humankind a unique mistake.

Maybe, we could restart with a better foot on the ground. Maybe, these ships would be the corpses of a lifelong lesson. Maybe, we would stick together like fire to heat.

Whatever happened on the ships would stay on the ships, never allowed to be discussed again. It was time to move forward, without questions.

ACKNOWLEDGMENTS

Thank you, Katie Chong, for working tirelessly as an editor. Your advice and edits have taught me many lesions throughout this journey, and I truly appreciate it!

Thank you, Elena Grantcharski for being such an amazing beta reader and editor. I appreciate all the feedback you have given me.

Thanks to my mother and father for giving me the tools to write. I am glad for the help you two have given me.

I would like to give a cute, little thanks to my cat, Safina. I love to write and have you beside me for the company. You would always find a way to distract me when I write, yet I can't ever complain about that.

Final thanks to you, the reader. I am beyond grateful that you chose this book to explore another world. I hope you enjoyed it.

Made in the USA
Columbia, SC
31 May 2020